DOCTOR WHO
PLANET OF FIRE

DOCTOR WHO
PLANET OF FIRE

Based on the BBC television serial by Peter Grimwade by
arrangement with the British Broadcasting Corporation

PETER GRIMWADE

A TARGET BOOK
published by
the Paperback Division of
W.H. ALLEN & Co. PLC

A Target Book
Published in 1985
By the Paperback Division of
W.H. Allen & Co. PLC
44 Hill Street, London W1X 8LB

First Published in Great Britain by
W.H. Allen & Co. PLC 1984

The BBC producer of *Planet of Fire* was John Nathan-Turner,
the director was Fiona Cumming.

Printed and bound in Great Britain by
Anchor Brendon Ltd, Tiptree, Essex

ISBN 0 426 19908 1

Contents

1

Mayday

The full fury of the storm hit the ship as it rounded the headland. Huge waves commandeered the trireme while gale-force winds strained against the efforts of the oarsmen to reach the land. Driving rain obscured the shore as Captain Antigonas tried to gauge the distance to the island harbour. They had shipped a lot of water and the vessel would need to be lightened if they were to reach dry land. The order was given to jettison the cargo.

The rich merchant Dimitrios instantly forgot his terror and nausea as he saw his treasures brought up from the hold. The marble statue was the heaviest single item so that would be the first to go. Six sailors grabbed hold of the carved figure, shrouded in sail cloth and splinted with strips of wood, whereupon an enraged Dimitrios rushed forward to protect the precious crate, with as much devotion as if the sculptured boy was his own son.

As the fat Rhodian fought with the crewmen, an enormous wave all but turned the boat on its end. The mariners grabbed whatever handholds they could while the cargo rolled to the lowered side of the deck. Unevenly ballasted, the ship was slow in righting itself and the sea poured in.

The Captain ordered the slaves to be released, for now it was every man for himself. As the half-drowned oarsmen struggled up from the flooded galleys, Antigonas offered a desperate prayer to Poseidon that he would live to see his homeland again. The next wave rolled right across the boat, yet still Dimitrios clung to his marble statue. The

Captain marvelled that a man should care more for a work of art than his own life. He peered closer at the stone image. Rough handling had torn part of the canvas away, revealing the head and shoulders of a young man—quite miraculously lifelike (and more likely to survive the day than his mortal shipmates).

By now several mariners were struggling in the water, some clinging to barrels, others striking out for the shore. But Dimitrios continued to embrace the marble boy, as if it were a lover. Then, as the ship rolled sideways, man and gilded kouros slid from the deck and plummeted to the ocean bed.

The storm hit the ship as it came into the gravitational pull of Sarn.

It was many years since any Trion vessel had landed on the planet, but the homing beacon was still in perfect working order as Captain Grulen programmed the flight computer for a fully automated re-entry through the atmosphere.

Grulen was looking forward to seeing Sarn. Several generations of his mother's family, so it was said, had lived there until the volcanos started getting over-active and the settlers came scuttling back to Trion from their colonial paradise, to complain endlessly about the climate and general short-comings of life on the home planet. (Not that Captain Grulen would be so unwise as to boast of any family connection with the Old Colonials.)

It must have been a surge of volcanic activity that caused the sudden magnetic storm. Whatever the reason, the navigational instruments took on a life of their own and the computer, deprived of accurate data, allowed their ship to enter the atmosphere of Sarn at the wrong attitude.

Within minutes, the ship was shaking violently

8

and the outer skin of the hull had heated almost beyond tolerance. The co-pilot tried to warn Trion Control, but with so much interference, radio contact was impossible and he could do no more than release the emergency data beacons.

Captain Grulen switched to manual operation and the ship swung slowly back into the right alignment for entry, but even with the retro-engines on full power, he knew they could never achieve a safe landing speed. He ordered the security quarters to be opened, for it was only right that the prisoners should take their chances with the crew.

There was no panic amongst Captain Grulen's special passengers. Faced with the daily prospect of execution, they had prepared themselves for death. One of the older men turned to the child beside him, sleeping peacefully in his mother's arms. He smiled and took his wife's hand in his. If this was the end, they would face it together and with dignity. His only concern was for someone far away on the Earth. What was to become, he wondered sadly, of Vislor Turlough?

2

Message Received

It was ridiculous, thought Turlough, that he should be so depressed. After all, the girl had been argumentative, tactless, interfering, brainless and with a voice that could strip paint. Perhaps it was just having no one to fight with, but he missed Tegan dreadfully!

So did the Doctor. He had grown accustomed to the humour, the courage and the sheer optimism of his Australian companion. They had parted friends, but she had been repulsed by the violence of his conflict with the Daleks, as if the horror brought by Davros's evil creations was somehow his own fault. He thought how easy it would be to stand back from the horrors of the Universe like the other Time Lords. Maybe he should do just that. After all, what good had his interference ever achieved? Even with Daleks! He turned to Turlough. 'I sometimes think those mutated misfits will terrorise the Universe for the rest of time.'

Turlough crawled from under the TARDIS console where he had been checking the stabilisers. 'Doctor, you're becoming obsessed.'

'Exactly,' repeated the Doctor. 'Obsessed and depressed.'

Turlough frowned. He had never seen the Doctor look so sad before. He decided to cheer him up. 'What we both need is a holiday,' he announced.

The Doctors spirits sank even lower at the idea.

'It could be fun.'

'Fun!' shouted the Doctor, who viewed the prospect of a vacation as only marginally less calamitous than the eruption of Krakatoa. 'There was precious little

11

fun when I went on holiday to Brighton. Unutterable chaos ensued.'

But Brighton was not at all what Turlough had in mind. Brighton, he imagined, would be just like Weston-super-Mare, where he had gone one wet half-term from Brendon School with his friend Ibbotson. He remembered how they had sat in Mr Ibbotson's Volvo, stared out at the windswept promenade, drunk tea from a thermos and eaten Mrs Ibbotson's weeping lettuce sandwiches. Ibbotson, of course, had been sick on the way back to school. If they were going to have a holiday on Earth—which was, after all, the Doctor's favourite planet—it would, Turlough decided, be on some paradise island. 'Do you the world of good,' he declared, scanning the TARDIS data bank for a likely destination.

'All right, Turlough,' replied the Doctor defiantly. 'I'll show you what holidays are like!' He began to set some co-ordinates. 'Only don't say I didn't warn you.'

As if on cue, a violent scream came from the inner TARDIS. Though of no human pitch or timbre, it was undoubtedly the sound of some creature in terrible pain. The Doctor and Turlough rushed down the corridor from the control room. The dreadful wailing grew louder as they approached the door of Kamelion's room. The Doctor had quite forgotten about the robot from Xeriphas, the former ally of the Master, who could assume more disguises than the evil Time Lord himself. It was some time now since Kamelion had declared himself the Doctor's obedient servant and taken up residence in the TARDIS. But the obsequious automaton had none of the cheerful loyalty of K9 and the Doctor always felt uncomfortable in the presence of this tin-pot Jeeves.

The Doctor pulled open the door to reveal

Kamelion lying spreadeagled on the floor, his silver limbs tense against some unseen assault on his nervous system. There was a shining aura around his metal body as if he was about to use his metamorphic powers to transform into a living creature. His speech transducer continued its agonised screaming. 'Help me...! Pain!'

For a moment the Doctor and Turlough just watched the tortured robot, unsure how to help. Then Turlough spotted the umbilical cord sneaking from the machine's torso to a junction box on the wall. Kamelion had connected himself to the TARDIS computer. Perhaps some feedback from the vast data system of the TARDIS had caused this derangement in the robot's own brain. Turlough leaned forward to break the link.

'No!' shouted the Doctor. 'We need the computer to stop the spasming. Go and programme an alpha rhythm.'

'Help, Doctor!' pleaded Kamelion.

'It's all right, Kamelion. Help's on the way,' comforted the Doctor as Turlough raced back down the corridor to the accompaniment of further cries from the robot's quarters.

The demented caterwauling gradually gave way to the soothing oscillation of an alpha rhythm as Turlough, back in the control room, followed the Doctor's instructions. Kamelion began to relax. He started to mutter deliriously. 'Point of contact... point of contact will be made...!'

The Doctor leaned forward, trying to make some sense of the rattling that came from the robot's throat.

'I am... obey... contact... me...'

'Contact who?' said the Doctor. 'What's happening?'

Turlough was about to leave the control room and

rejoin the Doctor and Kamelion when the signal came through on the communications unit—an urgent repeating modulation. 'Doctor, we're picking up a distress...' He stopped in mid-sentence, recognising something ominously familiar about the sounds from the console. He was sure he had heard it before—on a Trion ship.

Turlough's heart began to pound; the Custodians must have come searching for him. He listened again. It was a Trion ship alright... Perhaps in genuine distress? No, more likely a trick, he decided as he tried to detune the signal, for, if the Doctor heard it, he would be bound to track it down, playing right into the hands of his persecutors.

But the call sign repeated and repeated, obviously a broad-bandwidth transmission. Turlough glanced nervously at the open door of the control room. The Doctor could so easily walk in... Why wouldn't the signal stop! He grabbed the entire receiver module in both hands and forcibly dragged it from its housing.

The unit was silent; and so was Turlough, as he anxiously wondered where the transmission had come from.

The object of Professor Foster's curiosity lay in the box of pottery fragments that the divers had just brought up from the muddy sea bed. He had not immediately noticed the dumpy cylinder with its mushroom-shaped head, electing to sift through several large pieces of terracotta vase. These had been the first finds of the day from the ancient Greek merchant ship that lay five fathoms below the expedition boat moored in the bay.

Howard Foster was not in a hurry. The store room of the tiny island museum, like the boat itself, was already full of wine jars, jewellery, cooking pots,

14

coins and pieces of sculpted marble waiting to be transported to Athens. Soon he himself would have to return to America and write up the report of his work for the university. All the more reason to enjoy, while he still could, the sun on his back and the dappling of the morning light off the amazingly blue sea. It gave him the chance to recover from the irritations of a more than usually fractious family breakfast at the hotel.

He lifted the curious artifact out of the box. It was made of some hard, bright alloy unknown to the professor. 'Hey, Karl, come and have a look at this!'

His assistant turned from where he was labelling some shards on the other side of the deck. Joining the professor, he took the cylinder in his hand. 'Sure isn't Greek'. He traced, with his finger, the outline of two triangles, one half-laid over the other, that was engraved just below the bulbous head. 'Some sort of logo?'

Howard shook his head. 'Remember the Russian satellite that broke up last year?'

'You think this is from outer space?'

Howard shrugged his shoulders. 'Give it to the police when we go ashore.' Already he was losing interest. Whatever its provenance, the object was of no archaeological value. He could already see the launch from the harbour coming towards them; it was time to take the latest finds ashore.

Howard felt a sudden stab of annoyance. Beside a pile of oxygen cylinders in the centre of the approaching boat, and holding an animated conversation with one of the crew, was a young girl. What did Peri want now? He groaned quietly. It was not that he didn't like his stepdaughter—she was amusing, attractive, intelligent even. But try as he might to be friendly and pleasant, they always ended up arguing.

15

'Hi!' As the launch nudged up against the expedition boat, Peri jumped over the rail, a friendly grin on her sunburned face.

'What are you doing here?' It was not exactly a fatherly welcome. 'I thought you were off sightseeing with your mother?' As if he couldn't guess! Divide and rule had always been the policy of Miss Perpugilliam Brown, and doubtless, while her mother was out of the way, she wanted to sell him yet another hairbrained scheme.

'Mom's taken up with that Mrs Van Gysegham from the hotel.' Peri smiled innocently. 'And I'm not spending the day exploring a prehistoric cemetery with some octogenerian from Miami Beach.' She knelt on the deck and started sifting through the fragments in one of the boxes as carelessly as if it had been a pile of records in Bloomingdale's music department. 'That woman talks of nothing but the state of her large intestine. You did say come out anytime.'

Howard stifled his irritation at such a cavalier treatment of his as yet unclassified discoveries.

'Hey, what's this?' Peri lifted up the cylinder.

'I don't know.'

'That's never ... *platinum*?' Peri scratched at the metal casing with her thumbnail. She turned the flat-ended tube round in her hands with far more excitement than she had shown over the broken pots. Ancient Greek remains she could see any day, but here was something alien and unknown!

Kamelion had entirely recovered. 'I apologise for that hysterical display, Doctor,' he announced. 'For a moment there was ... confusion.'

'Are you all right now?'

'Of course.' The metal creature articulated

normally, with the bland, almost insolent, indifference of a speak-your-weight machine. 'Allow me to recompose myself, then I will try to explain the reaction I experienced.' Needless to say, Kamelion had no intention of doing any such thing, but being an automaton felt no twinge of conscience at the lie. He could not possibly discuss the crisis with the Doctor of all people! He must wait, listening for the signal... But what signal? He felt confused. *Any* signal! His memory circuits reiterated the distant summons... *'Contact must be made...'*

The Doctor returned to the control room trying to puzzle out what could have caused the robot's extraordinary seizure. 'Spasming's stopped and Kamelion's fully conscious,' he explained to Turlough. 'But I wish I knew...' The Doctor picked up the communications module that was still lying on the console. Several of the connector lugs had been bent in its rough removal from the housing. 'Turlough! What have you done?'

Turlough had been so desperate to silence the Trion SOS that he hadn't thought how to explain the damage when the Doctor found out. 'It was picking up some random emission,' he remarked casually, trying to think of a convincing reason for his vandalism. 'I thought it might be causing interference with Kamelion's circuits,' he added with a sudden flash of inspiration.

To Turlough's surprise and relief, the Doctor took his suggestion quite seriously. In fact he had frequently doubted the wisdom of allowing the automaton to transfuse so freely with the TARDIS intelligence systems. But the Doctor had still to discover the full extent of Kamelion's interference. 'Why have you reset the co-ordinates?' he demanded,

17

rather sharply, of his companion.

'I haven't,' protested Turlough.

'Well, someone has.'

'Kamelion!'

'He must have computerised the signal you heard.'

In which case, thought Turlough, the TARDIS is programmed for a one-way trip to disaster. If the Custodians were still in the transmission area ... 'At this rate Kamelion will have us chasing every random emission in the galaxy,' he blustered.

'Not quite,' replied the Doctor. 'Those co-ordinates are set for here on Earth.' He referred the configuration to the TARDIS data bank, then turned with a smile to his companion. 'You wanted a holiday, Turlough. We're now heading for your paradise island!'

The Doctor activated the rotor control. The central column began its slow rise and fall. Turlough felt doomed.

The blue box appeared amongst the shrub and rock of the deserted headland, as if to police some outpost of the Empire. But the arrival of the TARDIS on the distant point went unnoticed amongst the archaeologists on the boat in the bay, who were busy loading their precious treasures onto the harbour launch.

'Looks like Elton John,' said Peri, staring at the marble features of a young boy, who lay in one of the crates.

'Eros, if you really want to know,' replied Howard acidly, rather cross that the girl should be so facetious about his prize discovery.

'God of love and fertility,' declared Peri, just to remind her pedantic stepfather that she wasn't a complete ignoramus.

'Absolutely right,' said the professor, switching to

18

his seminar voice. 'A personification of natural forces in an anthropomorphic deity...'

Peri's eyes glazed over.

'In the same pantheon, Hephaestos represents fire, Poseidon the sea and earthquakes...'

Peri held up her hand to be excused the rest of the lecture. 'Howard, do you have to talk to me like I was the Albuquerque Women's League or something?'

Howard stiffened. 'If you are not interested...'

Peri wanted to scream. Why did the man have to be such a prima donna!

'I've got rather a lot of work to do,' muttered the archaeologist stuffily.

'Howard...' Peri gave her stepfather one of those looks.

'Or was there something else?' As if he needed to ask. The wretched child would hardly have come out just to make a nuisance of herself.

'No, no. You just get on with your work.' Peri flashed one of her Shirley Temple smiles. 'I only came to say hello...' She paused. 'And goodbye.'

'Goodbye? What are you talking about?'

'This island, Howard. I'm bored out of my mind.'

'How can you be bored for heaven's sake!'

Peri wondered how a few short words could explain that her stepfather's precious island, whatever it had been in days gone by, was now the plughole of western civilisation. 'For a start, there's no one here, under 65, speaks English...'

'There's Doc Corfield.'

'Doc Corfield's middle-aged!' (She would have added, had she been confident the gentleman was out of earshot, that Doc Corfield wore a hairpiece; and that was one of the first rules in the book of Miss P. Brown: never trust a man with a toupee!)

'Doc Corfield is *my* age,' her stepfather protested.

Peri grinned evilly, for Howard had exposed his

19

Achilles heel.

'Forty-one next birthday!' She put in the knife. And twisted it... 'Don't kid yourself you've found the secret of eternal youth with Levi cut-offs and a pair of sneakers.'

Howard could have killed her. 'So what do you want, Peri? Go to summer camp with a bunch of High School kids?'

'I want to travel.'

'Travel?' Now the girl was being ridiculous. 'You've been travelling all your life!'

'Sure I've been to the Athens Hilton, the Cairo Hilton, the London Hilton, the Ankara Hilton...' Peri decided she must stop her teasing before they both got involved in a full scale row. 'I've met a couple of really nice English guys and I'm going with them to Morocco.'

'Morocco?' So this was what it had all been leading up to. 'You're due back at college in the Fall.'

'That's three months, Howard.'

But Professor Foster had already decided how his ward's vaction should be spent. 'You've got your ecology project, your reading schedule, your exam revision... Come on, Peri, no way are you going to North Africa.'

'You can't stop me.'

'Okay. So what are you going to use for money?'

'Some of what dad left me.'

'That's in trust till you're twenty-one.'

'That's why I already sold my airline ticket.'

Howard was beginning to shout. 'How do you expect to get back to New York?'

'I'll get a job.'

'Don't make me laugh!'

'Please don't let's argue. I've made up my mind and that's the end of it.'

'Professor Foster!' Karl was waving from the

launch which was ready to return to the harbour. Howard walked to the rail, wondering how best to nip his stepdaughter's irresponsible project in the bud. He noticed how low in the water was the smaller boat with its valuable cargo. 'Let's go Spiros!' He jumped across to join his colleagues amidst the crates and boxes and the launch eased away from the side of the expedition boat.

Peri, who had not expected such treachery, rushed to the side. 'Howard!'

'Sorry, Peri. You'll have to wait for the next trip.'

'But that won't be for hours!' Already there was fifty yards between them.

'Mustn't be overloaded.'

'Get one of the crew to stay behind. There's a ferry at six ...'

'Sorry, honey.'

'You're doing this deliberately!'

Howard was smiling. 'I didn't ask you to come aboard.'

Peri was furious. How could he do this to her ... How could she *let* him do it?

'I will not be treated like this!' she wailed.

Howard gave a cheery wave from the disappearing launch.

'Of all the lowdown, cheap, rotten, sneaky tricks!' she screamed. 'You won't stop me Howard. You hear me!'

The view from the TARDIS scanner was positively idyllic: blue sky, blue sea, a sandy beach ... No evidence of any Trion activity. Turlough began to feel more confident. His hopes were dashed as the insistent, reiterating signal sounded again from the repaired communications unit.

'Is that the emission you heard before?' asked the

Doctor.

'It ... might have been,' prevaricated his companion.

'That isn't random!'

Turlough grew more depressed. There was no chance of stopping the Doctor once his curiosity was aroused.

'Sounds more like an SOS.' He hurried to the inner door. 'Get a fix on it while I have a word with Kamelion.'

The Doctor ran down the corridor and into Kamelion's room. 'Well, Kamelion. What do you make of it?'

'Doctor?' The robot cocked his head politely.

'The signal!'

'I hear no signal,' said the silver creature.

'You must do!' protested the Doctor, observing the cable that led from Kamelion to the connecting block on the wall.

'I am not capable of inexactitude,' lied his factotum.

'What about the other time? When you had your ... *confusion*?' said the Doctor, hoping for an explanation of the earlier occurrence.

'There has been no confusion,' replied Kamelion, blandly. 'My function has never been impaired.'

The Doctor stared into the unblinking eyes of the man-machine. Either the creature was being devious or there was a serious malfunction. He walked thoughtfully back to the control room to rejoin his companion, who was only too relieved that Kamelion chose to turn a deaf ear to the incoming signal.

'Did you get a fix?' asked the Doctor.

'There wasn't time,' replied Turlough, seizing on the most plausible excuse. 'The transmission stopped.'

The Doctor began to remove a small self-contained unit from the communications section of the console. 'If that signal transmits again, we'll get a fix on it with this.' Checking the temperature outside the TARDIS, the Doctor slipped out of his frock coat and opened the double doors.

'Wait while I go and change!' shouted Turlough. He slipped through the inner door, then under the pretext of going to his room ran up the corridor and into Kamelion's quarters.

Kamelion pivoted round as the boy came into the room. 'Take care, Turlough. It is very hot. With your fair skin you will easily burn.'

To the Doctor's anxious companion, the inhuman monotone of his voice seemed to turn the advice into a threat. He stared at the robot, wondering what two-faced game it was playing. 'The Custodians won't take me,' he whispered defiantly. 'I'm going to stay with the Doctor.'

'I do not understand your concern.'

'You heard the signal,' shouted Turlough angrily. 'You set the co-ordinates. You're helping *them*!'

Kamelion stared back at him, as inscrutable as a waxwork. Turlough felt a surge of rage—he was sure the robot was laughing at him. He leaned forward, grabbed the cable that linked Kamelion with the TARDIS computer, and pulled it sharply out of the socket. He turned back to the silver automaton. 'One word to the Doctor and I shall destroy you!'

3

Destination Unknown

The warm sun outside the TARDIS was a welcome
change from the grey chill of London and Turlough
found himself enjoying the walk along the edge of
the sea. As he sniffed at the scent of wild thyme and
mint and listened to the frantic midday chorus of
cicadas he began to put a more optimistic
interpretation on recent events. Perhaps it was no
more than a coincidence that they had picked up the
distress call of a Trion ship. Maybe Kamelion had
merely navigated the TARDIS to the ideal holiday
island.

Turlough slipped off his shoes and was soon
hopping around like a scalded cat on the red-hot sand.
He rushed to the water and paddled along in the
shallows. The Doctor strode more purposefully
along the beach, the detector in his hand, ready to
pinpoint the source of any further transmission.
Turlough wished heartily that the Trion ship,
wherever it was, would maintain radio silence.

It wasn't long before they reached the tiny fishing
village. A lorry was parked on the harbour wall, half
loaded with wooden crates and boxes, and a number
of large baskets were being hauled on a rope from a
boat tied up to the quay. An odd time, thought the
Doctor, to be landing a catch of fish. And the men,
struggling with the ropes in their designer jeans,
dark glasses and baseball caps made pretty odd
fishermen.

It was Turlough who first noticed the boxes of
barnacled amphorae. 'They're archaeologists,' he
exclaimed.

The Doctor hurried forward to examine the contents of the truck. His attention was immediately drawn to the marble statue of a young boy, lying in one of the crates. 'A kouros,' he explained to Turlough. 'Late classical period. Really rather fine.' Then for pure swank, he added: 'I would hazard a guess it's by a pupil of Praxiteles.'

'That's a remarkably well informed guess, sir,' came an American voice behind him. The Doctor turned and found his hand being grasped by the tall, bronzed man who had spoken. 'Professor Howard Foster,' the archaeologist introduced himself.

The Doctor congratulated the professor on his discovery. 'Pity about the erosion, though.' He indicated where the once finely chiselled lines of the artist had been blurred by centuries under water. 'But the effect is not unattractive. Like the Marine Venus on Rhodes.' A sudden idea came to him. 'Have you been working on the sea bed?'

Professor Foster nodded. 'The wreck out in the bay. She's a real mixed bag, like your English *Mary Rose*.'

The Doctor looked thoughtfully out to sea.

'Been nice talking to you.' The professor rushed away to supervise the lifting of the final crate from the launch.

The Doctor walked with Turlough towards the far end of the harbour wall. 'Suppose one of the divers disturbed something...' He gazed out to where the expedition boat rode at anchor over the wreck. Suddenly he began to squeak like an old lady who has turned her hearing aid up too high.

'Oh, no!' thought Turlough as the Doctor pulled the detector from his pocket. 'That signal again!'

'Just as I thought,' muttered the Doctor, squinting in the bright sunlight to get a reading from the device in his hand.

26

'It's coming from out in the bay. I wonder if we could prevail on one of the professor's divers...'

'That bearing's not accurate enough,' interrupted Turlough.

But the Doctor would not be discouraged. 'When the next transmission comes, we'll take one bearing from here and a second from the TARDIS. The convergence will give us the exact source.' He pointed to a small waterside café on the other side of the harbour. 'That will make an excellent base for the first radial.'

The Doctor hurried across the sleepy square, looking forward to a cool beer and a rest in the shade. 'Toss you for the TARDIS,' he offered, rather half-heartedly, to his companion.

'I'll go,' said Turlough, anxious to sabotage the Doctor's experiment. 'The heat is making me feel sick.'

Not even Ariadne, abandoned on Naxos, could have been so downright mad as Peri, marooned on her stepfather's boat. For a solid half hour she had walked backwards and forwards across the deck in a blind fury. Then, having nothing better to do, she curled up in the corner and fell asleep.

She woke up cramped, burned and hungry. After a fruitless search of the cabin for food, she felt all her anger returning. Howard had crossed her before, but never in such a humiliating way—in front of the entire unit! She looked at her watch. Her mother would still be on the other side of the island, her stepfather tied up at the museum for the rest of the day. If she could only reach the shore she could pack her rucksack in the hotel and meet Trevor and Kevin in time for the ferry.

If only she had been a strong swimmer. Yet it was a

27

mere half-mile to the nearest beach. The water was warm, and she could take it slowly. No problem.

Her mind made up, Peri stripped down to her swimsuit and stuffed her shirt and shorts into one of Doc Corfield's patent plastic bags he had conveniently left on the side of the labelling table. She was about to close the zipper when she noticed something smooth and gun-metal grey protruding from one of the boxes. It was the unidentified cylinder she had inspected earlier, cast aside and forgotten by the archaeologists. She picked it up. Hardly likely to be platinum, but the casing might be worth something as scrap. Finders keepers, thought Peri, and dropped it in the bag.

Sealing the waterproof satchel, she moved to the side of the boat, lowered herself into the water and struck out for the shore.

Nothing could have suited Kamelion's purpose better than to be left alone in the TARDIS. He waited patiently in his cubicle until the Doctor and Turlough had had time to get well clear of the time-machine, then, mobilising himself, he glided down the corridor and into the empty control room. He went straight to the console and patched his own circuits into the communications section where he began an extensive search of all the available frequencies. 'Contact must be made...' He still did not fully understand the problem, but he knew that his assistance was required urgently.

'Kamelion!'

The robot's head panned towards the intruder. How inconvenient of Turlough to return so soon. 'Contact must be made! Important to obey!' He shouted defiantly at the boy.

'No!' cried Turlough, rushing to pull Kamelion

away from the console.

It is a painful business rugger-tackling a robot, as Turlough discovered when the silver mannikin hurled him effortlessly to the floor. 'Do not interfere!' screamed the automaton monotonously. 'TARDIS will be taken to point of contact!'

Turlough didn't argue but crawled round the console out of sight of Kamelion. He could just reach the panel where he had previously programmed his electronic sedative. This time he selected a wave form that would do nothing for Kamelion's peace of mind or body.

The robot shrieked as Turlough switched on. High energy pulses flowed directly into his circuitry, blotting out all coherent thought and organised locomotion. His arms jerked and girated, smoke began to pour from his joints. With a final scream he twisted his body away from the console in a vain attempt to detach himself from the source of such crippling energy, and collapsed with an enormous crash to the floor.

Turlough leaned over the tormented automaton. 'You're not taking the TARDIS anywhere,' he boasted vindictively. 'And you won't be listening to any more messages. You're finished!' Slowly he dragged the the immobilised torso through the inner door, up the corridor, and dumped it, like a pile of scrap, in its own room.

Kamelion lay jangling on the floor, every system and circuit of his body in turmoil. Turlough rested against the wall while he got his breath back, then went out, slammed the door and walked back to the control room.

It did not take him long to remove all evidence of his attack on the robot, and he began to plan his stategy for the next Trion broadcast. He soon realised he need only falsify the reading and the Doctor would never get an accurate bearing on the radiation.

Turlough gave a casual glance up to the scanner. There was something in the water ... He zoomed the picture in. Just a girl swimming and waving at somebody on the shore. He zoomed tighter on the frantic semaphore ...

The girl was drowning.

It was dead easy, thought Peri, as she paddled herself confidently to the shore, towing the buoyant plastic bag behind her.

She was about half way to the beach when she felt the first stab of cramp in her left leg. Suddenly the water was colder, deeper, the shore more desperately far away than it had been when she left the boat. 'Don't panic! Don't panic!' she said to herself.

The convulsive pain shot to her thigh, twisting and unbalancing her whole body. She gasped, and sucked in a mouthful of seawater. She retched and spluttered, frantically trying to raise her head. She tried to wave, but there was no one to see her. She breathed in more salt water and choked helplessly. Her arms thrashed and splashed, her head went under and she could see white foam, a cold refracted sun. Air for a blissful second as she broke the surface, then down, down ...

Peri had no memory of Turlough's rescue. She just remembered the moment when she stopped struggling. The sudden peace. Was that what death was like?

'I think I'm going to die,' moaned Peri.

'No you're not,' said Turlough as he helped the half-conscious girl onto the bed in Tegan's old room.

The American lay back, exhausted, and closed her eyes. Turlough picked up her plastic bag from the floor. It looked as if there were some dry clothes inside. As he opened the fastener and fished out a pair of shorts and a shirt, a small cylinder rolled onto the bedclothes. Turlough grabbed it, and gazed at the object, his mouth dry, his heart thudding. It was a Trion data beacon. 'Where did you get this?' he shouted at the girl.

Peri's eyes flickered. 'Howard was such a pig . . . I needed the money.'

So that was where the transmission had come from—a beacon despatched from some stricken spaceship. Inside the cylinder would be the data core with all the details of the Trion vessel's location. It would have to be destroyed before the Doctor returned.

Turlough traced with his finger the engraved trefoil on the side of the cylinder. He rolled up his sleeve. There, on the inside of his arm, was branded the same overlapping shapes of the Misos Triangle. He stared at it bitterly. It was his stigma; the sign of humiliation and disgrace.

The detector on the café table began to whistle again. The Doctor picked it up and started to read off the bearing. Turlough had had ample time to reach the TARDIS and would now be computing the second radial which would enable them to tell within an inch or two where in the water . . .

'How odd!' The Doctor checked the reading. 'How very odd indeed!' He stood up, flung some coins on the table, and ran across the harbour square. He stopped at the corner and looked at the machine again. There was no doubt about it. The source of the signal had moved from the sea and was now very near the TARDIS.

Turlough was still struggling to unscrew the mushroom head of the cylinder when he heard the Doctor's footseps. He quickly hid the beacon in the towel with which he had made a perfunctory effort to dry himself.

'The point of emission moved,' exclaimed the Doctor as he joined his companion by the console. 'Good heavens! You're soaking wet.' He stared at the boy who was still dripping all over the TARDIS floor.

'Please, Doctor. Go and see Kamelion. He's had another fit,' said Turlough with as much urgency as he could muster. The Doctor said no more to his companion, but walked straight out into the corridor.

As soon as the Doctor was out of sight, Turlough gripped the bulbous head of the cylinder once more. At last the end began to turn and the thin wafer, protected by the tube, was soon in his hand.

'A data core!' said a voice behind him. The Doctor had returned from an all too brief examination of Kamelion and stood watching Turlough from the open door. 'You're right, Kamelion's in a bad way,' he said, without taking his eyes off the slither of silicon in the boy's hand. Moving to the console, he picked up the two pieces of outer casing from where Turlough had dropped them. 'A beacon,' he observed. 'Sent across space like a shipwrecked sailor's bottle . . .' He extracted the core from between Turlough's fingers. 'With a message in it. Who from, I wonder? And where?'

Turlough decided the time had come to confess his guilty secret. The Doctor must be stopped from contacting the Trion ship. He coughed nervously. 'Doctor, there's something I ought to tell you.'

Peri was dreaming again; the same recurring nightmare. She was a little girl once more, sent to bed in disgrace. 'Don't put out the light!' she pleaded with her stepfather. 'Please, Howard. Don't put out the light!'

Suddenly, there was energy. Kamelion could feel the restorative power in his circuits. 'Please, Howard . . . Please, Howard . . .' An irresistible force began to transform his now dazzling metal carapace. 'Howard! Howard!' The shining silver skin transmuted to a suit of sober cloth.

'Howard . . . Howard . . .'

The robot's burnished head transmogrified into the face of Howard Foster. The robot's new *alter ego* got to his feet, pulled apart his black jacket and white shirt, and plugged himself into the cable trailing from the computer outlet.

There was a flash and a puff of smoke.

'Oh, dear,' said the Doctor, who had been connecting the data core with the TARDIS computer system. 'Now we'll never know where the beacon came from.'

Turlough smiled.

'What was it you wanted to tell me by the way?'

'Doesn't matter,' said Turlough, much relieved.

The Doctor looked quizzically at his companion. The boy had been worrying about something all day. 'Anything wrong, Turlough?'

The interrogation got no further for the double doors abruptly, and quite spontaneously, slammed shut.

'Did you do that?' asked the Doctor.

'Of course not,' said Turlough, just as surprised.

The column began to rise and fall.

'The TARDIS has dematerialised,' exclaimed the Doctor.

'Kamelion!'

'Impossible. He's out for the count.'

Any further speculation on the destination of their mystery trip was cut short by the arrival in the control room of a smiling American in a dark, well-cut suit. 'Doctor, we meet again.'

The Doctor turned to the newcomer in amazement. 'Professor Foster!'

The robot, perfectly disguised, continued to act out the role of the archaeologist. 'This has to be the most amazing machine I've seen in my life.' He gazed round the control room in assumed astonishment.

'How did you get in here?' protested Turlough.

'I was following Peri,' drawled the duplicate professor.

'The girl!' cried Turlough. 'I forgot all about her.'

'What girl?'

'I was going to explain,' said a rather shamefaced companion. But he had left it a bit too late as the Doctor was already staring, nonplussed, at the inner doorway where a young lady in blouse and shorts stood blinking, equally amazed, at the mysteries of the TARDIS control room. '*That* girl, Doctor!' hissed Turlough in a loud stage whisper.

4

Crisis on Sarn

The sky above Sarn had been dark for seven whole days. Black rain had fallen on the fields. The earth had began to tremble and shake. A pall of smoke hung over the Fire Mountain. The darkness and the quaking ground had not come to Sarn for nearly a whole generation, and only the old people could recall the last days of endurance. From every corner of the ancient settlement, the citizens were hurrying to hear the wisdom of the Elders and the judgement of their Chosen One.

Timanov stared out past the crumbling columns of the elegant pagoda towards the smouldering mountain. Not for seventy years had he seen such a lowering prospect. At the last crisis he had been hardly more than a child. Now, he was Chief Elder of the Sarns, who would turn to him for guidance in the testing days ahead. Perhaps, he thought gloomily, his own misguided benevolence was in some way to blame for the hardship they were about to endure. He turned to the young boy at his side. 'Of course, in my father's time, Unbelievers were sent to the fire.'

'That was barbaric!' replied his companion, appalled at the brutal customs of the not so distant past.

The old man smiled. 'A little over zealous, perhaps. But in those days, Malkon, people did not tolerate dissidents as they do now.'

'The Unbelievers are harmless, Timanov.'

The Chief Elder looked uneasily at his young protégé. The boy had picked up too many liberal opinions. 'It is still a wise precaution to send an occasional freethinker to his death. A burning encourages respect for our traditions.'

The boy seemed nervous. 'I could never order a burning!'

Timanov sighed. He was fond enough of the child, but a Chosen One should be made of sterner stuff. He put his arm on Malkon's shoulder. 'You will be given strength.' The young man looked sad and frightened, overwhelmed by his responsibilities. 'Don't be worried, my boy,' continued the old man. 'It can be a most rewarding experience, and a blessed relief for those who are consumed in the flames. Doubters are such unhappy people.'

'Is it not sometimes good to doubt?' asked Malkon gravely.

Timanov was near despair. How could Logar have wished on them this milksop for a leader? How could this soft-hearted youth, with his scruples and his cringing sensitivity, be the child who had emerged from the Sacred Fire? He would need to be stronger with the boy. 'Come, Malkon.' He pointed towards the Hall of Fire. 'It is time for you to speak to the people.'

Malkon stared unhappily at the faded mosaic on the floor. 'Why me?' he pleaded, as he had pleaded a hundred times and more with his elderly tutor.

'It is the will of Logar, Lord of the Fire Mountain!' the old man cried. He drew back a corner of the boy's white robe and with his gnarled hand grabbed hold of Malkon's slender arm. The boy could not bear to look at the fateful birth mark, the two overlapping triangles branded into his flesh.

'You carry his sign,' the old man reminded him, You, Malkon, and you alone.'

Roskal and Amyand were very frightened. The

higher the two men climbed the hotter it grew and the more densely swirled the clouds of choking, sulphurous smoke. The ground trembled, there was an ominous rumbling and the two climbers looked fearfully towards the summit. For a moment they hesitated, appalled by the power that might, at any moment, be released, and in awe of their own audacity; for no man before had dared climb the Mountain of Fire.

'I can't breathe,' gasped Roskal. 'My feet are burning.'

Amyand was as terrified as his younger companion, but hid his fear. 'Perhaps Logar will be waiting with a cool drink and new shoes,' he joked nervously.

Loath to confront what lay above of them in the crown of black, fissile rock, both men rested for a while. The valley stretched beneath them—mile upon parched, grey mile of sterile pumice, calcinated rock and arid clinker. But it was not an entirely sombre view. In myriad strips of fertile soil, crops awaited harvesting and flowers of every colour bloomed. Across the valley lay the city, with its fine houses, paved streets and grand public buildings, which, though crumbling, had survived the destruction of every other settlement. Yet no one knew who had designed such munificence, least of all Amyand and Roskal, as they clung to the shaking slopes of the Fire Mountain.

'We must go on,' said Amyand.

Roskal nodded grimly. If they gave up now, nothing would stop the burnings and the human sacrifices to the Lord of Fire.

The last few yards to the summit were the worst. Smoking rock seared their feet and blistered their hands as they fought to haul themselves up, up... And on to the very rim of the smoking crater. They stood exhausted, gasping for breath. Before them was a vast saucer of smouldering ash. 'There's nothing there!' cried Roskal triumphantly.

'There's nothing there!' repeated his companion, and began to laugh with pure relief.

The Hall of Fire was one of the finest buildings in Sarn, its fluted columns, vaulted ceilings and marble pavements surviving the many earthquakes miraculously intact. Now it was filled with citizens, perturbed by the trembling earth, the darkness and the rumours of the all-consuming flames. Many of them were angry too, at the edict forbidding them to harvest their crops, and the old protocol that would not allow them to hide and protect themselves from the danger that was to come.

Sorasta looked out through the pillared transept, across the valley to the Fire Mountain. By now Amyand and Roskal should be on their way back to the Hall. Their testimony would bring to an end years of barbarity and superstition. The young woman spoke urgently to a group of men from her own street. 'Take as much food and water as you can store. We may be under ground for many days.'

'Unbelievers!' hissed an old greybeard.

'We must go to the caves,' shouted Sorasta defiantly.

The entry of the six Elders onto a raised platform at the end of the Hall silenced the arguments that raged in every corner of the assembly. Behind the six old men came Timanov himself, leading the timid, pale boy.

Malkon felt his mouth go dry as he stared at the sea of faces and tried to remember the lines the old man had rehearsed him. 'Citizens of Sarn,' he stammered. 'You have all seen the smoke from the Fire Mountain and the black rain, and have felt the quaking ground...' He tried to stop his own hands and feet from shaking. 'These signs tell us it is the Time of Fire.' He glanced over his shoulder at Timanov who gave him a curt nod. 'Logar, the Lord of Fire, is testing our faith,' continued the reluctant Chosen One.

'Testing our common sense!' heckled one of the young men from below. There was a murmur of sympathy from throughout the Hall.

Malkon wished he had words of his own to answer the Unbelievers, but he only knew what the old man had told him. 'Soon Logar will send a sea of fire from the heart of the mountain,' he declaimed mechanically.

'Then we must evacuate the city,' shouted another Unbeliever to a chorus of agreement.

'We must follow the tradition of our ancestors. We must show no fear,' persisted the boy. But the crowd was growing restless and the citizens were beginning to talk amongst themselves. 'We must not abandon our homes.' Malkon tried to go on, but angry voices opposed him everywhere. 'We must do ... *nothing*!' cried the boy, unable to believe his own words.

'What about our crops!' shouted one of the men who had been conspiring with Sorasta.

'Our crops! Our crops!' chorused the indignant Sarns.

Seeing that the tongue-tied Malkon had no answer, Timanov stepped forward and raised his hand. 'Leave them unharvested!' he cried. 'The fields must burn as an oblation to Logar and a measure of our faith.'

'We need bread not faith!' shouted one of the women contemptuously.

'You shall have both,' replied their Chief Elder.

The crowd grew silent, impressed by the weight of

39

Timanov's authority.

'Once in every generation our faith is put to the test. If we submit to Logar and are not found wanting, we survive and prosper. Then, as our reward, the Outsider will come.'

But there was still much doubt. For those who had grown up in prosperous times, it had been easy to pay lip service to the idea of being saved from the fire by an agency beyond Sarn. Now that they could *see* the smoke and darkness it was more difficult to accept. Perhaps the Unbelievers were right: that no one would guard them from the danger but themselves.

Timanov smiled. 'The Outsider will protect us. He will bring an abundance of good things. There will be food and many rich gifts...'

'No!'

The citizens turned from Timanov to the steps leading up to the columned hall from the street. Amyand and Roskal stood in the entrance. They were breathless and covered with black pumice dust. They were triumphant. 'It is a lie!' cried Amyand. 'There is no Logar!'

'Heretic! Unbeliever!' howled Timanov.

'We have climbed the mountain,' boasted the young man.

The crowd gasped and the Elders grew pale.

'It is death to trespass on the Mountain of Fire,' whispered Timanov.

'We have climbed and we live!' declared Amyand. 'For generations our people have been the slaves of fear. No more.'

Several of the crowd cheered. Amyand pushed his way through the excited citizens until he stood at the base of the stone dias. He stared straight at the Chief Elder. 'We have seen with our own eyes.' He turned again to the people. 'There is no Logar!' he cried.

There was more applause. The Elders were losing

control.

'If we are to survive on Sarn,' continued the young Unbeliever, 'we must learn to believe in ourselves and conquer the power of the Fire Mountain.'

Timanov strode angrily to the edge of the platform. 'Heretic!' he thundered at Amyand. 'You will burn for this!' But none of the guards moved. There was far too much sympathy for the Unbelievers.

'We will all burn unless we go to the shelters,' shouted Roskal from the centre of the assembly, to be answered by a roar of agreement.

'Citizens!' cried out Timanov, again. 'You cannot escape Logar's anger. He will pour his fire into your hiding places . . .'

Amyand jumped up to the dais, pushing the Chief Elder roughly aside. 'The old order is finished,' he jeered. 'Now we will live by reason and common sense.'

The Elders looked nervously from one to another, powerless to enforce their authority. Timanov looked around for the boy, but Malkon had retreated to the far end of the platform. It seemed they were lost. For their pride and disobedience, the city would be consumed in the flames that had destroyed all the other habitations. He turned to the Mountain, raised both arms in supplication and cried in a great voice. 'Oh, Logar! Send us a sign!'

There was silence throughout the Hall of Fire which was broken by a sudden roar. Flames began to burn behind Timanov's head. The Elders turned to the cave in the rock wall behind the raised platform, guarded by a rough iron grille. The grotto was filled with a raging fire. As the Elders staggered back from the heat, the ground began to shake, stones clattered from the walls and the distant mountain thundered. The mood of the crowd was changed in an instant.

41

Timanov looked into the fire and bowed his head. 'Logar, I thank you,' he whispered in profound gratitude. Once more the Chief Elder addressed the people. 'Citizens, I called to Logar and the Fire Lord has answered.'

The mountain roared again and the whole city trembled. Many of the citizens were on their knees. Timanov raised an accusing finger. 'To the burning with all Unbelievers!'

This time the guards did not hesitate. Amyand jumped from the platform, but the perfidious crowd blocked his escape. Together with Roskal and Sorasta he was dragged up the steps of the platform. One of the Elders flung open the gate of the cave. The three petrified Unbelievers recoiled from the heat of the flames that had turned the cavity into a furnace.

'Stop!' Amyand, struggling with the guards, made one last appeal. 'Only a Chosen One can order a burning.'

All eyes turned on Malkon.

Well, Malkon?' pleaded Amyand.

Malkon stared at Amyand, uncertain and afraid.

'Come, boy,' said Timanov sternly. 'Be strong. For the good of the people.'

'I don't know,' stammered the miserable child.

'Burn them! Burn them!' shouted the crowd.

'I cannot order the deaths of three innocent people,' protested Malkon.

'You call those heretics innocent!' spluttered Timanov.

'The Fire Lord requires sacrifice,' chanted the Elders in unison.

'Burn them! Burn them! Burn them!' roared the crowd.

Malkon was on the verge of tears. 'Remember what I taught you,' Timanov whispered in his ear. 'Resolution is everything. The laws of our people must be seen to be obeyed.'

The boy looked at the citizens, all now excited at the prospect of a burning; then back to the three frightened victims; and beyond them to the flickering fire. If only the judgement could be spared him . . .

'Malkon!' A man came running into the Hall. 'He is here!'

The crowd turned to the newcomer.

'With the sound of the great wind and a shining light,' cried the excited messenger. 'The Outsider has come!'

The TARDIS had materialised in a dark and dangerous land.

'A lot of volcanic activity,' observed the Doctor as he read off the inboard seismic scanner.

'Am I dreaming?' said Peri. 'Or will someone explain what sort of crazy ship this is?'

'How are you feeling, honey?' said the man in the dark suit who everyone believed to be Professor Foster.

'Sick!' answered the girl, unaware that she was conversing with a robot. 'Can I go back to the hotel?'

'Haven't you heard a word the Doctor said?' continued Kamelion in the guise of the American archaeologist. 'We're not on the island.'

'Then where are we?'

'I'm not sure,' said the Doctor, still examining the instruments on the console. 'But I'll get you back to Earth just as soon as I can.'

'Earth?!' screeched Peri, convinced that this Doctor needed urgent treatment himself, and wondering why Howard could take such raving lunacy so calmly.

'You're not going out?' said Turlough as the Doctor opened the doors.

'Why not?' said the Doctor, putting on his coat. 'The TARDIS decided to bring us here. I want to know why.'

The police box had landed in the centre of a large ruin. Only one wall remained standing, but a line of tapered columns marked the perimeter of what must once have been a very impressive edifice. Beyond the derelict building lay a desert of solidified lava.

'Reminds me of Pompei,' said the Doctor as he surveyed the scene from the door of the TARDIS. There was an ominous rumble and both looked towards the distant volcano.

'Pompei,' observed Turlough, rather pertinently, 'was utterly destroyed by the eruption of Vesuvius.'

But as usual the Doctor wasn't listening. He had wandered over to the corner of the ruin and was poking about the fallen columns and carved stones. Turlough ran across to join him. 'We shouldn't have left Kamelion.' He glanced nervously over to the TARDIS.

'Poor old Kamelion's virtually lobotomised,' grunted the Doctor as he pottered happily amongst the rubble.

Turlough said nothing. He had his own reasons for being afraid of the automaton, which he had no intention of discussing with the Doctor. The volcano grumbled like a sleeping giant with a touch of indigestion. 'That thing could erupt at any moment,' shouted Turlough, by way of encouraging a return to the TARDIS.

'Not according to the seismic scan,' replied the Doctor confidently and dropped to his knees. He fished the two halves of the casing from the beacon out of his pocket and peered at the carving on the side of one of the fallen pillars. He pointed to the symbol on the metal sheath and then at the engraved stone.

Turlough leaned forward. 'The Misos Triangle!'

he whispered.

'Someone or some *thing* must have computed the co-ordinates from the data core,' said the Doctor.

Turlough looked out across the miles of sterile black tufa, a nightmare landscape that had haunted his sleep every night in the cold dormitory at Brendon. So this was Sarn. He had tried so often to imagine what it might be like. When they read Dante with Mr Sellick he had thought only of this planet of fire. *Abandon hope all ye that enter here.* The poet might well have been describing this grim prison. 'There are people from Trion here,' he said quietly.

'Trion?'

'My home planet.'

'Why didn't you say so before?' said the Doctor, wondering why Turlough hadn't identified the double triangle when he first saw it on the beacon.

Turlough didn't answer. He was curious why the beacon had led them to Sarn, and what Kamelion's part was in it. At least there was no sign of the Custodians' ship. 'This is an old Trion colony,' he volunteered blandly.

'Very old and very deserted,' observed the Doctor, looking out at the empty horizon.

'Someone must still be here.'

The Doctor shook his head. 'That distress beacon could have been launched years ago.'

But Turlough was already running along the path that led from the ruin and out across the desert of ash and solidified lava.

Peri was trying to make her stepfather explain what had happened while she was asleep. She could see that her rescuer had taken her aboard a very remarkable ship. They had obviously been travelling. But away from the Earth?

Howard wasn't the least bit interested in Peri's questions as he perused the instruments on the control panel. 'The TARDIS is mine,' he muttered excitedly.

'Pardon?' said Peri.

'The TARDIS is mine,' said Howard more loudly. He operated a switch and the doors closed.

'Howard! What are you doing?' shouted Peri who knew quite well that her stepfather couldn't work a can-opener, let alone be trusted with machinery like this... 'Howard!'

But the man pressing buttons on the control console chose to ignore her protests. Lights flashed and alarms sounded.

'Don't touch that!' yelled Peri.

She screamed. Howard's face was slowly dissolving. The features of another man began to form in the halo over what had been the professor's body. The new face was dark, unsmiling, saturnine. It spoke in a new voice. 'I have succeeded. Contact has been made.'

'Who are you?' said Peri, frightened out of her wits.

The man who had materialised in the place of her stepfather chuckled evilly. 'I am the Master. You will obey me.'

5

A Very Uncivil Servant

Kamelion had enjoyed being Professor Foster. There was order, logic and (as one would expect from the survivor of so many Faculty purges) a vein of pure ruthlessness in the persona extracted from Peri's aura, that suited his purposes admirably. With all loyalty to the Doctor suppressed, he had begun to understand the nature of the emergency. As soon as he gained control of the Doctor's TARDIS he had paralleled the navigation unit with that of the other TARDIS. He could soon feel the now boosted metamorphic projection, and knew that he obeyed the supreme control. He began to think and see, move and feel, plot and plan like the distant Time Lord until the morphic plasma reformed and Kamelion *was* the Master.

'Is this some kind of trick?' Peri was stunned.

'Explanations are not necessary for you to help me with my work,' said the Master's metal familiar.

'Help you?' Peri began to feel angry. Like Alice at the bottom of the rabbit hole, she was about to pick herself up, dust herself down, and deal with life in the mad world on its own terms. 'I never asked to join this crazy outfit in the first place,' she protested.

The robotic Master continued to work at the console. Peri looked up at the screen and, to her dismay, saw Turlough and the Doctor—her only link with reality—disappearing into some desert. She tried to remember the lever Howard had used to work the doors. She edged forward . . .

But the Master had eyes in the back of Kamelion's head. Peri winced with pain as the black suited figure snatched her arm in his own steely hand. 'No, young lady, the doors will remain closed.'

'Don't touch me!' yelled Peri.

'You will remain in the TARDIS.'

Peri, who was unaccustomed to taking orders from strangers, aimed a sharp kick at the Master's shins that would have repulsed a Globetrotter. There was a howl of pain—from Peri. The man was made of titanium!

The Kamelion-Master transferred his hand to Peri's shoulder. As the hard sharp fingers sunk into her flesh, Peri screamed with pain and fear. The strength of her emotion was not lost on the robot. The same energy that had triggered his meta-morphosis into Howard Foster began to inhibit the Master's own projection.

Peri instantly noticed the look of discomfort on the man's face. She screamed again—and louder. Feeling his grip relax, she screamed some more. The Master's features blurred, his body glistened...

'Now what's happening?' Peri looked hopefully for the devil she knew to reappear. But there was nothing of Howard in the bald puppet that materialised in front of her.

'Who are you?' She stared at the authentic Kamelion. '*What* are you?'

The arms of the silver marionette jerked. A finger stabbed at the console. 'Help me,' said a little tin voice.

Only a genius of the Master's rank could have controlled the functions of his TARDIS entirely from the workbench of the laboratory, deep inside the time-machine. (Or so the Master told himself as he scanned the hastily assembled remote control units that operated the equipment in the console room.) The renegade Time Lord allowed himself a moment of relaxation. There had been a time when he feared Kamelion did not fully understand what was required of him. The metamorphosis projector, with which he now controlled the slave, had been an inspired invention, its design and construction— with materials available in the workroom—an achievement of epic proportions.

The Master observed with great satisfaction that his co-ordinates had been aligned with the Doctor's TARDIS, and turned to align his own head with the antennae of the new machine. He peered at the coherer with which he monitored the robot's morphic state. He snarled with rage. The round glass screen should have reflected his own image, but now he stared at the silver mask of the undisguised robot. Some interference—that girl!—had encouraged the creature to reassume its own identity. He increased the power of the projector, yet still Kamelion resisted. A robot that was not for him was against him. 'You will resist the girl!' he called. 'Her mind is strong, but you will obey only the Master.'

The Time Lord increased the radiation by a factor of ten, until the machine howled with the power surging through it, and the Master himself groaned with the pressure on his own brain. 'Kamelion! Kamelion!' he screamed. 'You will be the blind slave of my will!'

But the image in the coherer remained that of an unco-operative automaton. Kamelion must be transfusing with the Doctor's computer, the Master decided as he reduced power. There was no choice but to wait until he could use the projector at close range.

Kamelion felt himself grow stronger. He must be

loyal to the Doctor, help the Doctor's friend—and quickly! Not for long could he resist the demands of his other master.

'What's happened to Howard? Who was the other man? What's going on?' Peri plied the seemingly friendly robot with questions.

'Howard is safe on Earth,' Kamelion reassured her in a friendly voice. 'His appearance was a projection of your own energy which overwhelmed my personality circuits.'

'Circuits?' repeated the confused American. 'You really are some kind of robot?'

'I am Kamelion,' said the aristocrat of automata proudly. 'Was Kamelion,' he added in a sad voice, scanning his own neuronic damage. 'But I must help you...'

Neither of them saw, on the scanner, another pillar—a yellow, fluted Corinthian column—appear in the ruined colonnade outside the TARDIS. The Master had arrived.

A howl like an air raid siren came from Kamelion's mouth as he felt the increased radiation. He began to smudge.

'No!' shouted Peri. 'Please don't disappear.'

Kamelion struggled to hold on to a vestige of his own personality. 'An enemy of the Doctor is near,' he moaned. 'He invades me.'

'No, Kamelion! You're the only one who can help me.'

The girl's panic gave Kamelion the energy for a further moment of resistance. 'Leave the TARDIS at once. Find the Doctor...' He pivoted over the console and removed a small jagged wafer of printed circuit. 'Give him this. Warn him that the Master...' His words became an indecipherable ululation.

'The Master? Who is the Master?' Seeing that Kamelion could help her no more, Peri turned to the controls and fumbled with the door lever. Behind her someone chuckled. She looked back over her shoulder and saw, in place of Kamelion, the evil man in the black suit.

'My dear Peri,' the robotic Time Lord smiled. 'Do not be confused by my shifting appearance. The transfer has now stabilised. I am immutably the Master.'

In his adjacent TARDIS the real Master gazed into the coherer glass and saw his own image, as in a mirror. 'Excellent Kamelion. Now quickly. To my TARDIS. Release me.'

Obediently his *doppelgänger* opened the doors of the Doctor's time-machine and took hold again of Peri's arm.

'I'm waiting here for the Doctor!' shouted Peri, kicking and struggling.

'You will come with me,' hissed her tormentor, tightening his grip till Peri screamed, 'or you will remain in the TARDIS ...' he gave another chuckle ... 'dead!'

As they emerged into the ruined building where the blue police box had materialised, Peri momentarily forgot all her fears and discomfort at the sight of the ship's exterior. 'That's all I need,' she groaned. 'A flying closet!'

Her captor was about to add some observations of his own on the Doctor's substandard TARDIS, when the earth started to shake.

'Now what?' cried Peri.

'Merely the death throes of this blighted planet,' observed the Kamelion-Master, as he dragged his victim across the creeping ground.

'It's now or never,' thought Peri as she followed her leader for a few more deceptive paces, then, taking her cue from a further convulsion of the earth, sprung sideways. But the metal Master followed her every movement, tightening his grip on her arm until Peri begged for mercy.

The large stone which fell from the wall onto the creature's head missed the girl by inches. The Master's surrogate toppled like a ninepin and Peri was away, pausing only to dodge around a yellow, fluted Corinthian column which the earthquake was rocking alarmingly.

In the pitching laboratory, the Master struggled to steady his precious machine, but, as his TARDIS finally keeled over, both Time Lord and metamorphosis projector, with the whole paraphernalia of the workroom, tumbled like dice.

Outside, a second column crashed onto the fallen TARDIS, and a third amidst a shower of loose stones. Pediment and entablature from the derelict colonnade thudded into the growing pile of masonry.

The Master's TARDIS was well and truly buried.

The Master opened his eyes to find himself lying in the corner of his laboratory under a huge pile of equipment, his head aching vicariously from the blow to Kamelion. He got to his feet and looked round at the damage. The metamorphosis projector rested on its side in the centre of the wall which had now become the floor of the laboratory. The Master righted the machine, which was his lifeline with his slave. He breathed a sigh of relief for there was no sign of malfunction. A few adjustments to the controls and Kamelion appeared in the coherer glass in the image of the evil Time Lord. 'Excellent,' he whispered as he increased the power. 'Come, my Kamelion, revive!'

Kamelion clawed his way out of the mound of loose stones and mortar. He staggered to his feet and surveyed the general dilapidation. The Doctor's police box, he observed ruefully, was unscathed, while blocks of carved stone, columns, capitals, the lintel of a door were piled above and around the toppled, yellow, time-machine. The robot struggled for a while with the enormous chunks of masonry, but, for all his amazing powers, he was not Superman.

But his *alter ego* in the trapped pillar was not dismayed. 'Quickly,' called the Time Lord. 'Go to the Doctor's machine and materialise that preposterous box inside my TARDIS.'

The Master's other half hurried over to the blue police box and set the co-ordinates for the short journey while the Master speculated pleasurably on the Doctor's dismay at finding himself without the amenities of a TARDIS in such an uncomfortable corner of the Universe.

It should have been simplicity itself to navigate the undamaged time-machine into the buried console room, but although the lights on the control panel flashed while the column jerked and the whole console grumbled and groaned with effort, the Doctor's police box would not move.

In the nearby laboratory the Master was growing impatient. 'Why do you delay? Activate immediately!' he called.

'There is some malfunction,' the metal Master replied.

'There is always malfunction with the Doctor's TARDIS. Override the disabled units.'

The Kamelion-Master began to extract circuit boards from the centre panel and soon spotted the cause of the trouble. 'The comparator is missing!'

The Master gave a cry of anger. 'The girl must have removed it while my control was weak. You must find her before she rejoins the Doctor!' And he vowed that, come what may, the wretched child would die for her interference, marooned with the Doctor on the benighted planet of Sarn.

Peri had never seen a more forbidding place. The land was barren, devoid of colour, a slagheap that stretched as far as the eye could see. Smoke from the volcano on the horizon clouded the sky. If this was interplanetary travel she would stay at home in future.

She looked nervously back at the ruin. At least she had escaped that vile creature from the ship. There was a distant boom. Out of the frying pan into the fire, she thought morbidly, as the volcano rumbled. Unless she could find the Doctor and Turlough . . . With a stab of relief she spotted two tiny figures hiking across the black tufa, about half a mile away from where she had stopped to get her breath back. 'Doctor! Turlough!' she called. But it was a voice crying—quite literally—in the wilderness. The Doctor and Turlough continued, unaware of the girl's frantic efforts to attract their attention.

But Peri wasn't letting them out of her sight. She quickly abandoned the rough path that led away from the ruin to make a beeline for the distant explorers.

She soon learned the reason for the well worn track. What had appeared to be a gentle slope ended in a precipice. A deep ravine lay between her and the Doctor. Peri slithered to a halt, like a hang-glider pilot with second thoughts, on the edge of the drop. Several dislodged pieces of brittle rock and an avalanche of small stones cascaded over the cliff while Peri picked herself up and hurried back to the safety of the path.

The metal Master left the ruin in the opposite direction to that taken by the girl in whose pocket lay the vital comparator. The path followed by the robot led upward to high ground. Despite the loose rock and pumice the creature moved swiftly and had soon established himself on an excellent vantage point. As Kamelion looked slowly round, the Master's evil smile contorted his plastic features. In the far distance he could just make out the Doctor and Turlough, followed, some way back, by Peri who was half-way along the winding ridge path. The steep hillside between the young American and her single-minded pursuer would present no problem to a robot. He would intercept the girl before she caught up with the Doctor.

The Kamelion-Master laughed and started down the cliff.

Peri ran as fast as she could along the narrow ridge path, desperately trying not to lose sight of the Doctor and Turlough. As she hurried along she noticed other buildings beside the track, smaller than the ruin they had arrived in, but equally derelict. Clearly, this was not a healthy place to live and she couldn't wait to get out of it. 'Doctor!' She could see the man talking nineteen to the dozen with the rather sneaky boy who had pulled her from the sea. Why couldn't they look back for a moment!

The track led downhill for a short section, and, to her dismay, Peri could no longer see the Doctor and Turlough. She ran even faster, coming abruptly to a junction in the track. Instinctively Peri turned to the left . . . So much for female intuition! The new path ended almost immediately at a tumbledown gazebo perched on the cliff edge.

Peri had no time to admire any more ruins,

however picturesque, nor the splendid view of the valley, but she was intrigued to see a large brass telescope, mounted on a tripod in the tiny courtyard of the observation post. Perhaps there were people alive in this wilderness? She ran forward for a closer look.

The well polished spyglass was dust free and turned smoothly on its pan head. It was pointing back towards the ruin where the TARDIS had landed, and, as she looked through the eyepiece, Peri could see the blue police box and the fallen columns. No sign of the creature. She swung the instrument round hoping for a view of the Doctor and Turlough.

Something large and dark blurred across the lens. Peri fumbled for the focus. She slowly turned the knurled wheel, and in sharp perspective came the smiling face of the Master.

'My dear Peri!'

Peri leapt back from the tripod. The robot, in its least attractive shape, stood blocking the path.

'How positively evanescent you have become.' The creature was smiling sadistically. Peri took a nervous step back into the gazebo. 'In fact your disappearance has caused me a great deal of trouble.' The Master, still smiling, took a step forward.

'Keep away from me,' stammered the terrified American.

The smile vanished from the Master's face. 'You have removed a component from the Doctor's TARDIS.' In fact Peri had quite forgotten the tiny piece of circuitry that the friendly version of the robot had given her back in the ship. It weighed more heavily on the Master's mind. 'Give it back to me instantly!' he commanded.

The small, key-shaped wafer meant nothing to Peri, but she instinctively knew that, once in the hands of this odious man-machine, the Master would have some power over the Doctor and Turlough. And Peri needed the Doctor, in possession of all his faculties, to take her home. She edged towards a small wall at the end of the ruined belvedere. There was a sheer drop to the valley below.

The Master chuckled with pleasure at Peri's predicament. But Miss P. Brown did not give in that easily. She pulled the much sought after component from the pocket of her shorts and held it at arm's length over the parapet. 'Take one step nearer and you'll never get this back!'

The Kamelion-Master stopped in his tracks. He had not expected such defiance—least of all from a mere girl. 'If you damage the comparator, the Doctor's TARDIS is useless,' he warned.

Peri felt much better. The possession of this device gave her some bargaining power with the creature. 'Then keep your distance,' she retorted, starting to think she was in with a chance.

The Master, even as a robot, was not used to receiving orders. 'Give that component to me!' he blustered.

Peri stood her ground. 'This thing belongs to the Doctor. So it's the Doctor I give it to, or nobody.' She even managed to deliver the ultimatum with a Puckish smile—which enraged the Master.

'You will obey me!' he cried.

'Negative,' replied the recalcitrant Peri.

The Master could not believe such affrontery. 'I am the Master!' he declared, as if he were the Tsar of all the Russias. But this cut no ice with Peri who had been brought up on a college campus and was quite used to dealing with pompous little men who stamped their feet and behaved like spoilt children. 'So what?' she jeered. 'I'm Perpugilliam Brown and I can shout just as loud as you can.'

The Master was so angry that the robot all but blew

a fuse, and it was several moments before he could trust himself to speak. 'Peri, be reasonable.' He now used his velvet voice, adding an instant smile like a dab of lipstick. 'Without the comparator you can never return to Earth.'

The young American did not move.

'Do you wish to stand here until the planet is destroyed!' The Master was beginning to lose his temper again.

Peri was thinking fast. Somehow she had to break the stalemate. She remembered the effect that her anxiety had had upon the robot inside the TARDIS. Perhaps if she concentrated hard enough...

'Well, answer!' shouted the Master impatiently.

'Kamelion!' cried Peri, staring straight into the Master's eyes and willing the friendly robot to appear in his place. 'Come on, Kamelion. Show me your real self!'

'No!' The robot Master felt the power of her will and raised his hand across his face.

Peri was delighted; it was all in the mind. 'Kamelion! Kamelion!' she called, exalting in her new found influence. 'Kamelion! Howard! Anybody!'

The Master's features began to blur, his voice lost its human timbre. 'Resist... obey... resist... obey,' he repeated mechanically.

Peri could just make out the ghost of the genuine robot superimposed on the shimmering figure of the Master. 'Come on, Kamelion, you can do it,' she urged.

In the laboratory, the real Master was beside himself with fury. His own image had gone from the glass. Kamelion had succumbed to the power of the wretched stowaway from the Doctor's TARDIS. He tried to boost the metamorphosis projector. 'Kamelion,' he called. 'My slave! Resist! Have I travelled a billion light years through time and space to be thwarted by this brat?'

Kamelion did not answer.

'Resist the girl!' the Master screamed. 'Kill her immediately!'

Kamelion stood, shining impotently at the entrance of the gazebo. He was without motivation, identity or any recognisable shape, half-way between pure robot and metamorphic projection.

'Stay where you are, Kamelion,' whispered Peri, appealing to the machine's better nature. 'I'm your friend.'

But, friend or foe, Peri was keeping as clear as possible from the dazzling creature that still blocked the path to safety. She dropped behind some of the fallen stones and crawled, unseen by Kamelion, to the far corner of the ruined pavilion. Here the parapet had fallen away and gave access to a section of the cliff that was almost climbable. Mountain-eering had never been one of Miss Brown's accomplishments, but there was a first time for everything. With a glance back at the stricken automaton, Peri launched herself into the abyss.

6

Outsiders

Timanov insisted that the Watchman return with
him to the pagoda. As soon as they were inside
Malkon's apartments he pressed for more details of
what he had seen through the eye of the telescope.

'A sort of blue box,' said the young man.

'A blue box?' The Chief Elder shook his head.
'That's most unorthodox.'

But the Watchman was quite certain. 'A blue box
that came from nowhere,' he repeated. 'With a
flashing light.'

'There's no recorded history of a blue box,'
complained the old man. 'Still, I suppose all
Visitations are different.'

The lookout, who had a hearty dislike of all
liberals and freethinkers, gave a disparaging look
across at Malkon who was staring moodily out at the
view. 'Perhaps,' he whispered to Timanov, 'we have
been sent another Chosen One.'

Timanov gave a warning frown, but the pious,
young zealot had strong feelings on the matter and
was determined to speak his mind. 'This boy is weak.
The heretics walk free.'

'No Chosen One has appeared at the Time of Fire.
It can only be the Outsider.' Timanov shared the
younger man's sentiments and would willingly have
exchanged the callow boy for a more dynamic leader,
but it was not the will of Logar. At least the Fire Lord
had sent them his messenger. He smiled at the
Watchman. 'You are too young to remember, but
soon our storehouses will be full to overflowing with
the gifts of the Outsider.'

The three of them were joined by the other five Elders, now dressed in their finest robes. Timanov took a key from the cord round his waist and unlocked a large chest of some hard metal, from which one of his fellow Elders produced a silver rod for each man. Timanov smiled. The Elders would not be lacking in dignity when they met the Outsider. He turned to Malkon. 'We shall go to the place of arrival. In the meantime you have a chance to redeem your disastrous performance in the Hall of Fire.'

Malkon sighed. The events of the morning both frightened and bemused him. 'The Unbelievers do no harm,' he replied.

'No harm?' snorted the old man. 'That's the way they used to talk in the dead cities. And where are they now? Gone from the face of the land!'

Malkon was silent. He could not bring himself to believe in the intrinsic value of death and suffering.

'You must round up these Unbelievers,' continued Timanov, preparing to leave. 'We shall celebrate the Outsider's arrival with a great sacrifice.'

'No!' protested the unhappy boy. 'I can't!'

The Watchman, who was looking forward to a good burning, sneered at the Chosen One. He would be more than prepared to lend a helping hand. But Timanov already had the situation under control. The Chief Elder turned to the open door. 'Guards!'

Amyand, Roskal and Sorasta wasted no time in the Hall of Fire. Whatever the excited Watchman had seen through his telescope, they were grateful for the diversion and, as soon as Malkon intervened to order their release they were away down the colonnade, keen to put as much distance as possible between themselves and the flames in the cave.

They met no opposition in the deserted streets of

the city. The only danger was from falling stones. The ground, which had begun to tremble in the Hall of Fire, was now shaking the whole fabric of the city.

'The earth storm is getting closer,' cried Roskal to his two companions, as Amyand led the way down the street of empty houses, badly damaged in a previous disturbance. With a quick glance behind to see that no one was following them, they dodged into one of the large doorways and entered what must once have been a room in a large public building. Now it was open to the sky.

Together, they hauled back a large paving stone and Amyand helped Sorasta and Roskal onto the spiral staircase that led through the opening, down to an underground chamber. The cave was part of a natural fissure in the volcanic rock discovered by a group of Unbelievers just after the last bad quaking. Now, it served as a place of safety both from the earth storm and the orthodox zeal of the citizens. In one corner was a month's supply of food for the growing band of dissidents; in another there were blankets and mattresses.

About a score of men and women got to their feet as they heard the clatter of Amyand and Sorasta on the metal staircase. Amyand, still feeling scorched from the fire, explained what a narrow escape they had just had. There was much disappointment amongst the other Unbelievers, though not everyone had agreed with Amyand's daring plan to climb the Fire Mountain.

Roskal moved away to a far corner of the cave, curious to see the effect of the latest earth storm on the machine. That was another reason for keeping the cave a secret from the other citizens—machines were sacred to Logar and it was a burning offence to tamper with them. Not that any of the Elders were aware of the complex mass of apparatus with its dials, levers and flashing lights that some earlier inhabitants had installed in the cavern.

As the earth storm rumbled, the great machine appeared to have a life of its own. Roskal stood fascinated by the lights and sounds issuing from the weird contraption. He was sure this thing had been made by men like them. If only they could regain the lost knowledge—forbidden knowledge as it was now—they might yet learn to control the power of the mountain, as it was rumoured men had controlled it before.

After a while the trembling and rumbling began to die away. 'The storm is subsiding,' said Sorasta.

'Let's have a look outside,' said Amyand, joining Roskal by the machine.

There was one magical function of the mechanism that, by pure trial and error, Roskal had learned to control. He turned a switch and a view of the valley beyond the city miraculously appeared on a screen in front of him.

'Show us the Fire Mountain.'

Roskal obliged by moving another lever. The scanner began to pan across the dark surface of the land.

'Stop!' shouted Sorasta suddenly, pointing to the centre of the screen. The other Unbelievers crowded forward. Two men could be seen walking across the lava slope.

'Strangers,' exclaimed Sorasta.

'Impossible,' protested Amyand. 'They *must* be Sarns.'

There was agreement from the others, for it was known that all the other cities had been destroyed by the earth storms and the fires. It was the one area of history where they agreed with the Elders. There was Sarn and only Sarn in the whole wide world. There were no strangers, for all men alive were fellow citizens. Malkon peered closer at the screen. 'Look at their clothes!' Both men were dressed as no Sarn had ever dressed.

'Could they really be Outsiders?' suggested one of the younger Unbelievers nervously, to be answered by a noisy protest from his fellows at the hated word.

'No,' said Amyand. 'No one just appears by courtesy of Logar. They must be survivors from one of the dead cities.'

'We must talk to them!' cried Sorasta.

'You'll never get out of the city.'

But Amyand already had a plan. 'They're about to pass through the western col. We'll use the tunnel and cut them off.'

The Doctor did not like being so far from the TARDIS on such a treacherous and unstable planet. Urged on by Turlough, they had wandered further and further across the infernal landscape: white figures under a dark sky, trudging through black pumice drifts, like a negative snow scene.

The Doctor glanced anxiously at the volcano. ' "What if the breath that kindled those grim fires/Awakened should blow them into seven-fold rage/And plunge us in the flames?" ' he quoted.

'What did you say, Doctor?' asked Turlough, expecting at any moment, to be ordered back to the TARDIS.

'Milton,' said the Doctor. 'Didn't they teach you anything at that school?'

Turlough made a face.

'*Paradise Lost*,' continued the Doctor. 'I was thinking of our holiday island,' he added ruefully, gazing across a terrain that made the centre of Birmingham look habitable.

Turlough grinned. The Doctor didn't seem too

worried after all. Yet the boy felt guilty at encouraging his friend to explore so far. And he felt ashamed, now, of his cruelty to Kamelion. The robot was not involved in any plot, but had been instinctively following a distress call. And Turlough was grateful, because somewhere here...

'We ought to go back to Peri and the professor,' announced the Doctor.

'Please, Doctor, just a little further,' begged Turlough.

'But there's no one alive on this planet!'

Turlough pretended not to hear the Doctor and started to walk faster.

'You're in some kind of trouble aren't you, Turlough?' said the Doctor catching up with the boy.

'Of course not,' answered Turlough defiantly.

The Doctor looked his companion straight in the face. It was time for an explanation of the young man's strange behaviour.

'Hey!' In that desolate land the voice seemed, at first, to sound in their own heads. 'You there!' The Doctor and Turlough turned to the blackened hillside. Half-way up the slope, two human figures, dressed like Bedouins against the dust, were waving at them.

'We've found them!' shouted Turlough, rushing to the slope. He scrambled up the steep clinker like a crazed animal, scattering pumice and cinders in all directions and sending up a great cloud of dust. The Doctor waited for the shock waves to die down and followed in a more dignified manner.

Amyand stood in the entrance of the narrow hillside tunnel watching the boy's approach. Both the boy and the man who followed him were indeed strangers to Sarn, the first unknown faces the two natives of the city had ever seen. Amyand leaned over the edge and hauled Turlough onto the hard floor of the tunnel. Turlough was breathless and choking from the lava dust. The Sarn looked at the young man with intense curiosity. He was just like himself.

'You're safe,' gasped Turlough. 'We found your beacon,' he added, still helplessly out of breath.

The words made no sense to Amyand who helped Sorasta to haul the second stranger up into the entrance of the passage. Neither of the two Sarns had any experience of talking to people they did not know. 'You are welcome, strangers,' said Sorasta haltingly.

Turlough got to his feet. 'Are there any more of you?' he asked anxiously.

Amyand nodded. 'Our group is sheltering in the bunker.'

'Why didn't they send a rescue ship from Trion?' asked Turlough indignantly.

'Trion?' said Sorasta uncomprehendingly.

'The home planet,' said Turlough impatiently. 'You *are* from Trion?'

Amyand and Sorasta looked blankly at the boy. 'We are from Sarn,' said Amyand, suddenly finding the obvious amazingly difficult to explain.

Turlough looked at the two inhabitants of the hostile place in acute dismay. Who were they if not his own people? And where were the Trions? The man had spoken of a group. Perhaps they would know something of his fellow country-men. 'There must be Trions here *somewhere*,' he protested.

The only answer came from the volcano which rumbled ominously in the background. The Doctor was starting to get worried. He wanted to get well clear of the place before the inevitable cataclysm. But there were people here who faced certain extinction if they were not helped. Why did he always have to get involved, he wondered for the second time that day.

They hurried through the dark cracks of the hillside like rodents navigating the secret byways of the skirting board. The underground tunnel was damp and smelt faintly of rotten eggs. As they walked, Amyand and Sorasta tried to give an account of life on Sarn. 'The Elders manipulate Malkon,' explained Amyand.

'He's our Chosen One,' added Sorasta.

'Free thinkers are persecuted, contact with machines is forbidden.'

Turlough shook his head, unable to understand what these primitive people were doing in the old Trion colony.

'Timanov and his friends live off their tithes without an honest day's work in the fields,' continued Amyand.

'Logar pays well,' said Sorasta bitterly.

The Doctor was sorry, now, that he had left Professor Foster in the TARDIS. This would be right up the archaeologist's street: the power of the mountain turned into a fire god, human sacrifices . . . The ground trembled very slightly and the Doctor turned his attention to the more immediate problem. 'Unfortunately,' he explained to their guides, 'no amount of burnings are going to prevent the destruction of your city.' He looked around the tunnel and whispered to Turlough: 'Of course you realise we're actually walking in one of the vents of the volcano.'

There was a light ahead of them and in a few moments the Doctor and Turlough stepped from the narrow fissure into the cave which sheltered the other dissidents. The new arrivals, shading their eyes from the sudden glare of the torches, were instantly surrounded by the Sarns, like missionaries amongst a group of South Sea Islanders.

The excited Unbelievers first stared, then touched,

and, as they lost their shyness, fired salvo after salvo of questions at their unexpected guests. The Doctor tried to explain to the awestruck Sarns that there were worlds beyond their known world, civilisations beyond the city of Sarn, a whole universe of *other people*.

There was a sense of exultation amongst the Unbelievers. Their doubts, their speculations, their intuition, their inchoate struggling towards the truth had been validated by the testimony of this Doctor. The stranger also shared their fears of the volcano, but not unfortunately their choice of hiding place.

'When that volcano blows,' said the Doctor, looking round the cave and wishing he had taken a more accurate reading of the TARDIS seismic scan, 'molten lava will pour in here and burn you alive.' There was consternation among the Sarns. 'I have a ship...' said the Doctor rather hesitantly, wondering how many more Sarns there were above ground who would need to be evacuated in the TARDIS. He needed Turlough's help.

The Doctor's companion, who had ignored the previous conversations, looked up from his examination of the machinery in the corner of the cave. 'A seismic energy converter,' said the boy. 'For powering the city.'

The Doctor was very impressed. 'Built by your people?' Turlough nodded.

'Very old,' observed the Doctor, examining the controls. 'Your fellow Trions have long since abandoned the city.' Turlough said nothing.

Amyand turned to the Doctor. 'This ship of yours...'

Turlough had not heard the Doctor's tentative offer of transport and didn't like the idea at all. 'We can't turn the TARDIS into an orbiting refugee camp,' he whispered aggressively.

'Oh, I see,' said the Doctor angrily. 'Trions we help, Sarns we abandon. Quite a little racialist at heart, aren't you?' He glared at the boy. As Tegan had never been slow to point out, Turlough could be a rather nasty piece of work.

Turlough groaned; the Doctor had entirely misunderstood him. But how could he explain to the Doctor that they must find his own people before the real holocaust began? 'These are primitives, and we've nowhere to take them,' he blundered on.

'I suppose you prefer the final solution of the volcano!'

What was threatening to become the most serious argument the two of them had ever had was interrupted by the rattle of feet on the metal staircase from above. A young Sarn who had been keeping an eye on events in the city jumped the last four steps into the cave. 'Timanov has left the city,' he announced breathlessly. 'They're all crowding into the Hall of Fire. The Outsider is expected at any moment...' He forgot what else he had to report as he caught sight of the two strangers.

There was much jeering from the Unbelievers at the idea of the old men going out on such a wild goose chase, but Amyand did not join in the laughter. He remembered how excited the Watchman had been when he arrived in the Hall of Fire. The man had obviously seen something. He tried to remember the lookout's words. 'A shining light... The sound of a great wind...'

'Sounds a bit like the TARDIS,' said the Doctor obligingly.

'The Watchman wasn't lying,' exclaimed Sorasta.

'That old fox Timanov is going to have a hard time looking for the messenger of Logar.' Amyand laughed and pointed triumphantly at the Doctor. 'Because *we* have the Outsider here!'

70

7

The Misos Triangle

The six Elders of Sarn trudged wearily along the ridgeway path like a procession of Desert Fathers. 'I could wish,' said Timanov, sweltering under his ceremonial robes, 'that the Outsider had contrived his arrival a little nearer the city.'

The Watchman led them straight to the lookout point from where he had spotted the blue box. As they approached the ruined belvedere, the old men suddenly stopped. They cried out with sudden joy and all fell to their knees. In front of them, between two broken columns of the pavilion, stood a man suffused with unearthly radiance.

The Master, trapped inside the buried TARDIS, was near despair. He had lost control of Kamelion who was stuck, half-way between his robotic and metamorphic state. He glared angrily at the shining image in the coherer glass. He could even feel the sense of confusion in the mind of his *alter ego*, but he was powerless to break the inhibition. It was all the fault of that girl. But she would live to regret her interference . . .

The Master's hands moved swiftly to the controls of the metamorphosis projector. Something was happening to Kamelion. 'There is energy around you,' he called to the stranded automaton. 'Use it!' He boosted the machine to the overload threshold and groaned as the power went out of himself. 'Come, my slave!' he cried. 'Be at one with me!'

Kamelion, glittering like a Maltese tinfoil Saint at

71

Festa time, turned slowly to the six old men prostrate in the dirt before him.

'Welcome to our city, Outsider,' said one of the old men in a trembling voice.

'Who are you?' asked the robot.

'Timanov, Chief Elder of the Sarns.' His outstretched arms shook. Tears filled his eyes. 'I have struggled to keep the faith alive.' He looked up at the seraphic figure. 'I never thought I would live to see this day, but Logar is just...'

The Master laughed. 'We shall use these superstitious fools.' He gazed at the coherer which now gave back the true image of the renegade Time Lord.

The Elders gasped as the radiance died and revealed a stranger in a dark suit. A complete Outsider.

The Kamelion-Master, secure again in his identity, was more than willing to be escorted to the city, where he was sure to find the girl Peri and the Doctor, to whom she would have gone running with the comparator. His old enemy was in for a considerable surprise.

'We have grown lax with our observances,' said Timanov penitently as they walked back towards the city. 'But all that will change. There will be regular burnings.'

The protestations of loyalty from the Elders delighted the Master and he smiled, for the prospect of burnings pleased him mightily. 'You must root out the enemies of Logar,' he exhorted the Chief Elder, turning to take hold of one of the old men's staves. (He could only guess how laser guns had come into the hands of primitives but he would enjoy explaining their proper use.) 'There is one supreme enemy...' the Master chuckled. 'He calls himself the Doctor.'

It was a mistake, the Doctor decided, to have left Professor Foster in the TARDIS. He would have appreciated the archaeologist's company walking in the ancient streets of Sarn, and he would have relished the connoisseur's opinion of the faded grandeur of this desert metropolis. It reminded him (the professor would surely have agreed) of the old Roman city of Ephesus, with its crumbling stones and quake-toppled columns—the face of imperialism made acceptable in elegant decrepitude.

Turlough, who must have known something of the colonial history of his forebears, said nothing throughout the journey from the bunker to the Hall of Fire. The Unbelievers were also silent, nervous that any moment some zealous citizen might come forward to denounce them.

The Doctor and Turlough with Amyand and his group of dissidents halted in a side street just beyond the main entrance of the Hall. Amyand nodded to his men who drew swords and knives from under their clothes.

The Sarns assembled in the Hall of Fire thought for a moment that the Elders had returned. But none of those arthritic ayatollahs could have achieved the speed with which Amyand's picked men dashed up the portico steps and into the Hall.

'Don't anyone move!' shouted the rebel leader as each Unbeliever ran to his strategic corner, grabbed a citizen and held a knife at his throat. 'Stay where you are and no one will get hurt.'

The guards raised their sabres, but dared not move for fear of causing injury to the hostages.

Amyand ran to the stone platform in front of the cave where the fire still raged. 'You're here to see the Outsider,' he shouted, giving the crowd no time to recover from the shock of the invasion. 'Well, you won't be disappointed—because we've found him for you.' He gestured to the entrance as the Doctor arrived at the top step of the portico like a royal bride. 'In fact, two of them!' cried Amyand excitedly as Turlough joined the Doctor.

The citizens were overawed by the spectacle. Like the Unbelievers, they had never seen strangers before.

'Doctor! Turlough!' Amyand saluted the aliens who, escorted by the two armed Unbelievers, processed through the Hall, every eye upon them. 'Do they look like messengers from Logar?' shouted Amyand. 'They're men like us!'

It was a disconcerting experience for the Doctor and Turlough to walk from one end of the building to the other under such universal scrutiny. Turlough was so embarassed that he had no inclination to look round the Hall, and it was not until he reached the platform by the cave that he saw the units from the Trion ship. 'That's the navigational unit from a Trion space shuttle!' exclaimed the boy. 'And the concentrator from a propulsion unit!' He pointed to another piece of hi-tech pseudo-sculpture that adorned the platform.

'These people,' continued Amyand, pointing to the Doctor and Turlough, 'will tell you that Logar is dead—that Logar never existed.'

Turlough, however, was not interested in the idealogical problems of the Sarns; he wanted to know what they were doing with bits of a Trion space ship. But there was no chance to start asking questions as several of the more elderly Sarns had begun to protest at their treatment from Amyand's gang of iconoclasts. One of the hostages had managed to free himself and several of the guards seemed on the point of a counter coup.

'Stop!' The voice that echoed through the hall was shrill and immature, hardly more than that of a child. Turlough felt a sudden sense of *déjà vu*, as if he and the boy, now entering with Sorasta, had met in some previous existence. Malkon walked confidently to the platform, 'There will be no fighting. I order you to put down your weapons.' Reluctantly the guards obeyed. Malkon took the Doctor's hand. 'You are welcome to Sarn.'

The Doctor smiled. 'Not a very hospitable planet at the moment.'

'You will hear out this Doctor,' said Malkon, feeling far happier with the friendly newcomers than with the bullying mullah, Timanov.

While the Doctor tried to explain to the Sarns the danger of the molten lava that would shortly erupt from the volcano, Turlough crept forward to get a closer look at the components from the ship. His expert eye easily identified the age and classification of the vessel. He also noticed, on the side of the navigation unit, the ominous but unmistakeable signs of burning. 'Where did you find this?' he unceremoniously challenged the boy that Sorasta had called their Chosen One. 'Tell me, please!'

This was a question that Malkon had asked Timanov many times. Somewhat apologetically he now gave the same answer. 'That is a gift of Logar.'

'These things came from a Trion spaceship!' shouted Turlough accusingly. 'Where did it land? Where are the crew?'

The Doctor, who had joined him beside the components, seemed particularly interested in a large module in the navigation section. 'Whoever the benefactor, he's provided you with a transceiver unit,' he observed.

'What is a transceiver unit?' asked Roskal curiously.

'A way of communicating with other people,' replied the Doctor, wondering if there was a way of avoiding so many refugees in the TARDIS. 'People who can take you away from the city before it is destroyed.' He turned to Turlough. 'If we can get a message through to Trion, they can send a rescue ship...'

'No!' screamed the boy, pulling the Doctor's hand away from the transmitter. 'Contact Trion and you'll ruin everything!'

The Doctor was rapidly losing patience with his companion's eccentricity. 'Are your compatriots so inhospitable?' he demanded.

How Turlough now wished he had swallowed his pride and explained his predicament to the Doctor the moment he had heard that first transmission from the ship's distress beacon. 'The Custodians will move in,' he stammered. 'Escape will be impossible.'

'What are you talking about?'

Turlough did not hear the Doctor's question. He was staring, mesmerised, at a silver pendant on Malkon's neck. 'Where did you get that?' His finger pointed accusingly at the object.

'It is nothing,' answered the young man, startled at such intense interest. 'A Chosen One has many gifts.'

'There are more like this?' cried Turlough.

'Of course.'

'Show me!'

Exasperated as he was with his companion's behaviour, the Doctor was dismayed to see him leaving the Hall, together with the nominal leader of the Sarns. He didn't fancy organising the embarkation of the entire citizenry single-handed. 'Turlough!' he shouted after the retreating boy. 'I need your help.'

Turlough gave a guilty look back at the Doctor, but did not stop. 'You don't understand,' he shouted. 'My father was on that ship!'

Malkon took Turlough straight to his apartments

in the pagoda where the Doctor's companion instantly recognised the burnished metal case in which were kept the gaudy items that the Elders had presented to their Chosen One. 'A bonded flight box!' he shouted, forcing open the lid of the container to reveal a jackdaw's nest of stolen pieces.

'All these objects are from a Trion ship,' exclaimed Turlough as he dipped into the gimcrack treasure-chest and selected three tear-shaped drops of platinum, each on a thin wire chain. 'The identity tabs of a shuttle crew!'

'I don't understand,' said Malkon, perplexed. 'Where did they come from?'

Malkon shrugged. 'I have had them since I was a child.'

A wild suspicion inplanted itself in Turlough's mind. 'Malkon, where do *you* come from?' he asked the boy.

'I come from the fire,' answered Malkon simply.

Turlough's suspicion grew stronger. 'Why do they call you the Chosen One?'

'I carry the mark of Logar.'

'Show me.'

As Malkon pulled back the sleeve of his tunic Turlough gave a small cry. 'The Misos Triangle!' On the younger boy's arm was branded the motif from the cylinder and Turlough now knew where he had seen Malkon before. 'Take me to to the fire where you were found!' he shouted.

Malkon was appalled. 'Impossible. That is forbidden land. Trespassers are sent for burning.'

'I order you,' said Turlough defiantly.

Malkon scowled. 'No one can order a Chosen One.'

Turlough rolled up the sleeve of his shirt to reveal the same double triangle, seared on his upper arm. 'Except another Chosen One!' he whispered to the startled child.

77

There was great excitment in the Hall of Fire when the Doctor switched on the transceiver he had found in the ornamental wreckage. The Doctor, however, was less enchanted than the childlike Sarns by the babbling atmospherics that came from the communications unit. 'We need more power,' he muttered, wishing Turlough was there to lend a hand with repairs.

Sorasta, who had been keeping an anxious vigil at the entrance steps, pushed her way through the curious crowd towards the stranger in the frock coat. 'Doctor!' she called nervously. 'The Elders are coming.' There was a buzz of excitement from the citizens who couldn't wait to see what the old men thought of this self-confident alien.

'Good,' said the Doctor, hardly bothering to look up from the dismantled components. 'I need to talk to them. We've a full scale exodus to organise.'

When Moses came down the mountain to find the Israelites dancing around a golden calf, he must have looked something like Timanov as he strode through the Hall of Fire towards the impious stranger who was desecrating the precious relics. 'Seize the enemy of Logar!' shouted the white-haired patriarch. 'Arrest all Unbelievers!'

The Doctor got to his feet, beaming his cheery vicar's smile. 'Look, we're here to help you. That volcano could erupt at any moment.'

Timanov glared at the supreme heretic. 'You must be the Doctor,' he hissed. 'It is the Outsider's wish that you go to the fire.'

The Doctor sighed. A lot of explaining would be needed to get these superstitious people onto the rescue ship. 'There is no Outsider,' he began patiently. But Timanov wasn't interested. He nodded to the Elders. The old men pointed their staves at the enemy and the Doctor found himself staring down the muzzles of five deadly laser guns. A young rebel, unimpressed by a mere rod held in the shaking hand of an elderly man, stepped forward to protect the ally of the Unbelievers.

'No!' shouted the Doctor.

But he was too late. A ray stabbed at the young man who fell lifeless to the ground. The crowd gasped at this terrible new power. The Doctor stared, horrified, at the body of his protector. Who could have explained to these unsophisticated old men the violent purpose of their regalia?

The crowds turned towards the entrance again; someone else had come into the Hall. It was a tall, sinister man in a black suit. The late arrival chuckled darkly.

'Oh, no,' said the Doctor quietly. 'The Master!'

8

An Enemy in Disguise

The ship had split, on impact, into three parts. Two sections had been so badly burned as to be unrecognisable, but the third was easily identified as the flight deck. Turlough stared at the shattered instruments and twisted controls—it was amazing that anyone could have lived after such a crash. He walked across to the tail section where Malkon stood gazing at the charred, half-dissolved skeleton of the ship. Volcanic dust had collected in drifts against the distorted bulkheads, some alloy in the hull was slowly corroding in the sulphurous air and had bled a lurid green and yellow across the superstructure.

'This was your sacred fire,' said Turlough to the young boy. 'A crashed ship.'

'A ship,' repeated Malkon thoughtfully. 'Did I really travel from Trion in *this*?'

Turlough nodded. He had tried to explain to his companion as they hurried across the valley and over the ridge into the forbidden land, that the mark of Logar on his arm branded him a citizen of Trion, Turlough's own home, not this planet of fire. 'It must have been spectacular,' he added grimly, thinking of the ship hurtling in from space, red hot with friction, engines screaming against the inevitable impact. He imagined the explosion and the massive con- flagration from which a baby had crawled alive. A miracle indeed, but not quite as the superstitious Sarns had interpreted it.

'Where are the others?' said Malkon.

Turlough had been asking himself the same question. If Malkon had survived, why not the passengers or the crew? Could they still be in hiding somewhere?

He moved to the clearing between the three hulks. There was a circle of small stones, around which a few ragged flowers brightened the scorched earth. Malkon walked across to join the elder boy who was staring at the ground.

'Turlough?'

Turlough turned roughly aside. He did not want his new friend to see him weeping.

Peri was hopelessly lost. 'Doctor! Turlough! Anybody!' she wailed, desperately scanning the vista of clinker and dust. She was cut and and exhausted by her terrifying scramble down the side of the ravine, and hot from her trek through the sterile valley. She was thirsty, she ached all over, and she was very, very frightened. She held back another wave of blind hysteria and tried to work out the direction of the Doctor's blue box.

There was something on the horizon that was not made of rock and lava. As she got closer, she could distinguish girders, struts, a body of metal and—she could have cried with relief—two human beings.

'Hey, Turlough!'

A dishevelled Peri staggered towards Malkon and Turlough as the two boys emerged from the shadow of the wreck.

'What are you doing here?' said Turlough as the girl collasped on the ground.

'Thank goodness I've found you,' she moaned. 'I was beginning to think I was the last of the Mohicans.' Sitting up, she caught sight of Malkon. 'Who's this?'

'Malkon,' said Turlough impatiently, wanting to know why Peri had left the TARDIS. 'Another traveller,' he explained to Malkon.

'Hi,' said Peri, hoping that Malkon was the ordinary, uncomplicated teenager he looked. She got to her feet. 'Oh, boy. Have I seen everything today! A transgalactic payphone, a stepfather who turns into a robot...'

Turlough grabbed her arm. 'What did you say?'

'A robot who turns into some hoodlum...'

As Peri continued her tale of woe Turlough began to piece together what must have happened in the TARDIS. It was so obvious. The real professor had never really left the island—it was Kamelion all the time.

'That's him,' agreed Peri. 'But I sure prefer the Tin Man to this Master.'

Turlough's blood ran cold. 'The Master?' he cried. 'Kamelion turned into the Master?'

Peri nodded, massaging her bruised shoulder.

The horrified Turlough couldn't imagine what had made the Master usurp the robot and bring them all to this Trion colony. But he now realised he had left the Doctor in the most appalling danger.

It was a rare joy for the Master to see the dismay on the Doctor's face as he entered the Hall of Fire. The pleasure was enhanced by the knowledge that the youthful Time Lord had been totally duped by his own robot. He soon found himself enjoying the adulation of the crowd. Deification, he decided, was no more than his due. Nor would he disappoint his worshippers.

'Wretched citizens of Sarn!' he thundered at the congregation in the Hall like a hell-fire preacher. 'You have turned your backs on the Lord of the Fire Mountain and listened...' He pointed an accusing finger at the Doctor, 'to his enemy!'

The Doctor struggled in vain to explain that this

Outsider was no more than a traveller, for the crowd was enthralled by the evil automaton.

'On your knees, miserable people,' cried the Kamelion-Master. 'Abase yourselves before the messenger of Logar.' And his audience obediently fell to their knees and abased themselves.

'The man's an imposter!' shouted the Doctor.

The Master's surrogate laughed. 'Save your breath, Doctor, to tell me where is the girl from your TARDIS.'

'Peri?' said the Doctor, who had never doubted that his American passenger was safe with her stepfather in the time machine.

The Master was puzzled by the Doctor's genuine surprise. 'She has joined you here,' he prompted, impatient to regain the vital TARDIS component. 'Where is she? Where is the comparator?'

The Doctor's mind raced. What had been going on in the police box while he was exploring with Turlough?

Timanov bowed before the man in the dark suit. 'Let us hurl the enemy in the flames, Outsider.'

'Not yet.' The Kamelion-Master smiled. The Doctor would surrender the comparator before he died. Meanwhile, the rebels, befriended by his adversary could satisfy the bloodlust of the old men and perhaps encourage the Doctor to be more co-operative. 'Burn the others first!' He waved dis-missively in the direction of Amyand, Roskal and Sorasta. The Elders raised their staves and the guards marched forward, grabbing the three Unbelievers.

'No!' shouted the Doctor, as the three Unbelievers were frogmarched to the cave where the fire still raged.

Once more they sought judgement of the Chosen One.

'Malkon is not here,' sneered the the Chief Elder. 'It

is the will of the Outsider that you all die. The messenger of Logar has supreme authority.'

The Doctor watched helplessly. The Master laughed and whispered in his ear: 'The comparator, if you please.'

'I don't *have* the comparator,' protested the Doctor. 'Where is the girl?' he pleaded. 'What have you done with Professor Foster?'

'The professor has been eliminated,' announced the Kamelion-Master, learning at once, from the agonised look on the Doctor's face, that Peri had not yet found the Time Lord to give her account of the robot's activities—or to hand over the comparator. 'Such an absurd capacity for distress.' He mocked the Doctor's concern for his passengers in the police box, though of course that inadequate machine was now inoperable without the comparator. But, no matter. Here was an army of slaves to evacuate his buried TARDIS.

'Continue the burning!' ordered Timanov from beside the cave. The guards dragged back the heavy iron grille from the entrance.

'Help us, Doctor!' screamed Roskal and Sorasta. But there was nothing the Doctor could do. Two young Unbelievers ran forward in an impulsive bid to aid their comrades, but even before the guards could grab them, the Elders raised their staves and the youths were felled by deadly rays. The Doctor lowered his head at the carnage.

'You are quite powerless,' jeered the Kamelion-Master, 'and since you do not have the comparator, entirely dispensable. You may join your friends in the incinerator.' He called once more to Timanov. 'Continue with the burnings, Chief Elder. See that this Doctor burns slowly!'

The old man turned towards the mountain. 'Great Logar!' he cried. 'Receive these mortals as an oblation from your faithful people.'

The flames burned even more brightly and the Elders raised their lasers to drive the Doctor and the Unbelievers into the cave.

'Journey's end, Doctor,' said the Master. 'I'm sorry your cremation will deprive me of our periodic encounters.' The words of valediction over, he gestured to the guards. 'Quickly, my time is short.'

'No!' shouted the Doctor as he was manhandled towards the fire. 'You know the laws,' he cried in a desperate effort to gain time. 'A burning cannot take place without Malkon's consent.'

'I overrule the Chosen One,' said the would-be Outsider dismissively. 'Do not delay!' he barked at the Elders.

The crowd were so enthralled by the spectacle at the cave that the arrival of Turlough, Malkon and Peri at the entrance of the Hall went entirely unnoticed. Turlough peered from behind a pillar towards the martyrs' cave, where the Doctor was on the point of execution. 'What are you waiting for?' he hissed at Malkon. 'Get in there and stop them!'

'But I'm a Trion, not a Chosen One,' protested the confused child.

'They don't know that,' shouted Turlough, and pushed Malkon out into the crowd. He grabbed Peri by the hand. 'Quickly,' he whispered, dragging her back to the portico.

'We can't leave the Doctor,' complained the girl as she stumbled down the steps into the street.

'I think I know how to stop the fire,' cried Turlough, running as fast as he could in the direction of the bunker.

'Stop!' Malkon marched bravely through the crowd. 'There will be no sacrifice.'

All heads in the crowd turned while the Elders and the guards froze—to the fury of the Master. 'What are you waiting for?' he shouted. 'Continue the burnings!'

Still no one moved.

'That man is an imposter!' Malkon pointed to the metal Master.

'Who is this boy?' raged the false Outsider, furious at the delay.

The Doctor, making the most of Malkon's timely interruption, pushed aside the guards and turned to his enemy. 'Don't you know?' He gestured towards the young man. 'Allow me to introduce Malkon, Chosen One of the Sarns.' Giving the Master no time to reply, the Doctor moved to the Elders. 'You see,' he continued, anxious to discredit the Time Lord, 'this so-called Outsider doesn't even recognise your leader. And he doesn't understand the laws of the city.'

The old men mumbled uneasily amongst themselves, each one reluctant openly to defy the Chosen One. They looked towards their Outsider for some sort of lead.

The metal Master, inadequately briefed, blustered like an actor unsure of his lines. 'Obey me, or there will be no gifts!' He raised his arm towards the mountain. 'I will call down the wrath of Logar on you all!'

The Elders looked at Timanov. 'The boy is overruled,' he announced arbitrarily. 'Continue the burnings.'

'No!' Malkon stepped forward to protect the Doctor. One of the old men raised his laser, the ray darted like a snake's tongue, and the boy fell senseless beside the flames.

The Doctor groaned, the crowd gasped and the Elders stared in horror at the Sarn who had dared to take the life of a Chosen One. Only the Master was unmoved. 'Never mind the boy. He has sided with my enemies. It is Logar's will that he should die.' He pointed impatiently to the cave. 'To the fire with the Unbelievers!'

The fire promply went out.

There was an awful silence, broken finally by the voice of Timanov. 'Logar refuses the sacrifice.' He turned accusingly to the assassin. 'He is angry that his Chosen One was struck down!'

Turlough and Peri ran as fast as they could down the narrow streets, praying that they would not lose their way in the half-ruined city.

'That kid won't hold them off for long,' said Peri, who had no idea what the Doctor's companion was up to.

'There!' Turlough had spotted the derelict building and dashed forward into the open courtyard where he stared tugging at the stone. 'Help me!' he called to the girl.

'Looks like Houston Control,' exclaimed the American as they descended the metal stairway to the bunker.

'Older, but hardly as crude,' said Turlough, ever contemptuous of Earth technology. He hurried to the control panel of the machine. 'It's part of an ancient flow system,' he explained as he scanned the knobs and dials he had scrutinised earlier. 'If I hit the right circuit...' His fingers hovered over the green button on one of the side decks ... 'I can cut the gas supply to the cave.' He stabbed hopefully at the regulator. As he withdrew his hand from the switches, Peri noticed his fingers were crossed. 'Let's have a look.' Turlough transferred his attention to the surveillance unit. A view of the Hall of Fire appeared on the screen where Roskal had first spotted the explorers from the TARDIS.

'You've done it!' yelled Peri as she caught sight of the dark, unlit cave.

Turlough grinned, feeling rather pleased with himself. 'Second rescue of the day,' he thought. But the Doctor wasn't out of danger yet. They could see him arguing with the imitation Master, and at the mercy of five menacing laser guns.

'Seems like the Doctor could use some help,' said Peri, already rattling up the spiral staircase.

The Doctor and Amyand knelt beside the body of Malkon in the entrance of the cave. 'He's not dead,' whispered the Doctor with relief as he felt the faint pulse. He glanced towards the shocked and demoralised Elders. 'But let them think he is,' he added, anxious to exploit the confusion caused by the Chosen One's apparent demise.

The boy stirred. 'Warn the Doctor...' The Doctor leaned lower. 'Kamelion...The Master...' he muttered feverishly.

The Doctor cursed himself for not taking Kamelion's odd behaviour in the TARDIS more seriously. It should have been obvious—the Professor had been a robot all along. And so was the Master!

He got slowly to his feet, planning his next move. The danger was still very real. The man in the Burtons suit might well be no more than a sophisticated machine, but he embodied the mind, the will and the evil purpose of the renegade Time Lord, who even now must be watching him through Kamelion's eyes. 'You're not the Master at all,' he challenged the would-be Outsider. 'It's not even a man, it's a thing! A machine!' he proclaimed, to the whole assembly of the Sarns.

The *thing* snarled.

'We can fight it,' the Doctor shouted to the startled

trio of Unbelievers. Just concentrate your minds on destroying it.'

'A mortal destroy the Messenger of Logar?' replied the angry voice of the Master. 'Impossible!' The black-suited robot rounded furiously on the Chief Elder. 'Kill these insolent heretics!'

For a fleeting second the Doctor caught the robot's eye. The creature turned defensively from the Time Lord's knowing gaze. 'Don't look away, Kamelion,' commanded the Doctor. 'You will accept my will,' he continued hypnotically. 'I am the Doctor ... You are mere metal, base, deadweight, solid ...' The robot's jacketed arms began to flap like semaphore flags as the Master's persona struggled with the authentic Kamelion. 'You're a mass of printed circuits. You're Kamelion ... Reject control!'

A gurgling came from the creature's throat. 'Will you allow my enemy to torment me?' gasped the Master's voice, while the Doctor continued his remorseless evocation of the true Kamelion.

'You're no more than the sum of your parts, a million minature bits and chips ...'

'Kill him ...' The Master was choking.

'He likes killing,' said the Doctor bitterly. 'He reneged on your Chosen One. Next time it will be you, Chief Elder.'

Timanov did not know which way to turn.

'Kill!' spluttered the Master.

'Logar must decide,' said Timanov with the wisdom of Solomon. 'Let the Fire Lord give us a sign.'

'You'll have a sign alright,' cried the Doctor, confident now that he could demolish Kamelion's evil control. 'If we break the link with the Master, your so-called Outsider will be nothing but a heap of spare parts.' He spoke again to the automaton. 'You're on your own, Kamelion. Your control is

90

weakening, turning to silver... Silver puppet jumping on a string...' The creature's body jerked. 'String cut!' snapped the Doctor. The Master groaned. 'Stricken mannikin,' continued the Doctor mercilessly. 'Broken toy... No more playing the Grand Panjandrum!'

The Doctor smiled. The Master had started to fizz. The pure Kamelion was about to break through. The citizens were astonished. 'The shining! The shining!' they cried.

'I don't believe it,' whispered Roskal, appalled.

'Psychomorphic fringing,' said the Doctor without taking his eyes off the now radiant figure. 'Nothing supernatural about that. It's an intermediate stage between anthropoid and robotic identity.'

He might as well have been explaining disco dancing to a party of Carmelite nuns. The crowd saw and believed in the divine inspiration of the Outsider's shining. 'It is Logar's sign!' cried an elderly woman.

The Doctor was oblivious of the frenzy of the citizens. 'We're winning!' he shouted at the Unbelievers.

'Doctor, we're playing into their hands,' warned Amyand. 'The more you attack it the more it looks like the Outsider.'

But the Doctor knew the control was about to break. 'Keep concentrating! It won't be so impressive when it's a mere robot.'

In the laboratory of his TARDIS, the Master also knew that the fragile link with his servitor was all but severed. But the Kamelion's sensors had revealed to the stranded Time Lord a power within the Hall of Fire that was invisible to the eye of the Doctor. 'The cave!' he gasped, staring at the refracted image in the glass. 'Quickly. Shield yourself from the Doctor, in the cave!'

'You're becoming Kamelion,' droned the Doctor mesmerically. 'Obey me ... The Doctor ...'

A disembodied voice cried from the dazzling shape. 'Take them to the cave!'

'Obey the shining one!' ordered Timanov.

'Don't resist,' whispered the Doctor as he allowed himself to be shepherded with Amyand, Roskal and Sorasta into the grotto. 'Any distraction will allow the Master to break through.' The Doctor showed no dismay as the grid across the opening slammed shut. An obedient Kamelion would soon release them.

The Doctor was stunned to see his old enemy reform instantly at the cave entrance. The metamorphic Master surveyed the prisoners behind the bars. 'Doctor, you quite let your enthusiasm run away with you.' He laughed at the humiliation of his adversary.

'What went wrong?' asked Amyand, crestfallen at the sudden reversal.

'Something in the cave is screening the thought control,' muttered the Doctor, angry with himself for not forseeing the possibility.

The Master grabbed a laser gun from one of the Elders. He smiled, almost fondly, at his greatest enemy. 'Over the years I have dreamed a million exquisite tortures to accompany your final moments, Doctor.' He shook his head sadly. 'That it should come to this.' He raised the slender rod towards the horrified Doctor.

'Stop!' A girl's voice echoed from the entrance of the Hall.

The Master spun round to see Peri pushing her way through the crowd towards him.

'Peri, get back!' shouted the Doctor.

But the courageous American marched steadily towards the man in the dark suit. 'Kamelion!' Peri chided the metal Master as if he were a disobedient puppy. 'You're supposed to be the Doctor's friend!' The Master smiled. 'Kamelion!' repeated Peri with slightly less confidence. But there was none of the fringing she had so easily triggered, back on the ridge path.

'You see,' the Kamelion-Master laughed. 'I have grown stronger since our last meeting. Your puny mind can no longer effect me.' He took a few steps towards her, his hand outstretched. 'I am grateful, however, that you have seen fit to return the comparator.'

'That thing is where you'll never find it,' answered Peri, immenseley relieved she had handed the component to Turlough on the way back from the bunker.

'No matter.' The robot Master nodded to one of the Elders who raised his staff in the direction of the young girl.

'No!' protested Timanov. 'There has been too much killing.'

There was authority in the Chief Elder's voice that worried the Master as he gazed at the image in the glass of the metamorphosis projector. He felt resistance coming through the feedback system. 'Do not oppose them or the TARDIS will never be free,' he warned his other self. 'Take the girl with you. She is unskilled but strong. We will use her.' As for the Doctor, he was reluctant to allow his scheming rival out of his sight, but he must not risk alienating the superstitious Sarns with an orthodox execution. And the Doctor would be safe, locked in the cave, dying in the final holocaust that would soon destroy Sarn and all its inhabitants.

'Very well.' The Kamelion-Master shrugged. 'Spare the girl. I have work for her.'

The Doctor knew that without Peri's intervention he would now be dead, and he was horrified that she was, once more, at the Master's mercy. 'Leave her,' he pleaded from the cave. 'She is no part of our quarrel.'

The Master was delighted to see the pain he caused his enemy. 'At least in my TARDIS she will be spared the paroxysms of this dying planet.' A warning rumble from the volcano synchronised with another evil chuckle from the Master. 'I am sorry to be deprived of the pleasure of seeing you die, Doctor.' He smiled through the bars. 'Though I am consoled by the thought that your imminent and inevitable demise will be excrutiating!' He turned abruptly from the cave. 'Now, Chief Elder, I have work for you all, elsewhere.'

'Work?' protested the old man. 'But where are the gifts? The Outsider always brings gifts from Logar!'

The Master could see the Elders muttering suspiciously amongst themselves. With so much at stake he would need to be scrupulous in observing their bizarre protocol. 'Of course,' he reassured them. 'The gifts. I have them in safe keeping at the ruin . . . Buried!'

Turlough watched from behind a pillar as Timanov, after a brief discussion with the surrogate Master, explained to the citizens that they were all to go to the ruin where the blue box had materialised. From his hiding place Turlough saw the Master, his metal hand tight around Peri's wrist, lead the Elders to the entrance. The girl gave one last, frightened glance back towards the prisoners in the cave. The Doctor waved reassuringly.

With a cruel laugh, the Master dragged the young American down the steps of the portico, while the chattering crowd began to follow the Elders out into the streets and towards the outskirts of the city.

Inside the cave, the Doctor turned wretchedly from the entrance. Suddenly he held up a hand. It was sticky from where he had been gripping one of the

94

cross bars of the grid. He sniffed the rust-like deposit and moved to the wall of the cave. 'I knew something more than rock was screening me from Kamelion.' He searched in his pocket and produced a small penknife with which he began to scrape at the stone.

A shadow fell across the entrance of the cave. 'Turlough!' cried Amyand.

The boy put a finger to his lips and pointed to where several citizens were still leaving the Hall. The Doctor joined his companion at the grid. 'What kept you?' he asked, rather sarcastically.

'I've been to my father's ship.'

The Doctor frowned. That young man had a lot of explaining to do. But for the moment they had to get clear of the cave and after Peri.

'Hurry up, Turlough,' said Roskal. 'The flame could return at any moment.'

'I doubt it,' answered Turlough, struggling with the bolt which was fixed tantalisingly out of reach of anyone inside the cave. 'I've rerouted the flow from the bunker.'

The Doctor gave his friend a grateful smile as the gate swung back. Amyand and Sorasta went immediately to the prone shape on the edge of the stone rostrum.

'Where's Malkon?' said Turlough to the Doctor. His friend looked anxiously over to the kneeling Unbelievers. 'Oh, no!' cried Turlough, as he recognised the child whose head was propped up on a bundle of clothing. He rushed to the injured boy and knelt beside him. 'Who did this?' he asked bitterly.

'One of the Elders.'

'I shall kill him!' said the boy in a cold, matter of fact voice.

'What good would that do?' The Doctor put his hand on Turlough's shoulder, surprised to see his companion so upset. 'We've got to get after Peri.'

'You don't realise!' said Turlough, gazing down at the unconscious child. 'Malkon is my brother.'

9

In the Heart of the Volcano

As they carried Malkon along the abandoned streets towards the safety of the bunker, Turlough told the Doctor of how the child had guided him to the wreck of the ship in the forbidden lands. The Doctor listened in silence as his companion described how he had seen the graves of the passengers and crew. The boy was still very upset, otherwise the Doctor would have pressed him with many more questions about his family's fatal journey to the hostile planet. 'Who could have buried the victims of the crash?' he asked tactfully.

'The Unbelievers?'

The Doctor nodded. He could imagine the dissidents creeping out by night to inspect the smouldering hulk, discovering the Trions and realising the truth about the fire. 'Why don't Amyand and his friends know more about the ship?' he asked thoughtfully.

'The place of fire is out of bounds—on penalty of death. The people who buried my father must have got caught.'

The Doctor shuddered. He remembered how close he had come to such a burning. Turlough looked down at the body of his brother as they turned off the street into a derelict house. 'Savages!' he muttered.

'He was very lucky,' said the Doctor, leaning over Malkon as Amyand and Sorasta laid him on one of the bunk beds in the corner of the cave. 'The power cell in the gun must have decayed.'

'Will he be alright?' asked Turlough pathetically, as he kneeled beside the bed.

7

'I don't know. He's in severe shock.' The Doctor tried to sound more hopeful than he felt. 'There could be some damage to his nervous system.'

Leaving Sorasta to look after the injured boy, the Doctor moved over to the machinary in the other half of the cave. He was curious to know more of the technology of the old Trion colonists. 'Why fuel that cave with volcanic gas?' he muttered as he scrutinised the flow system.

'The cave has always been used for sacrifices,' said Roskal helpfully.

'With all due respect to your fellow Sarns, the people who built this had a more sophisticated purpose than burned offerings to Logar.'

'Ready, Doctor?'

The Doctor turned from the ancient switches and dials to where Amyand stood waiting for him in the entrance. Turlough jumped up from Malkon's bedside. 'Don't you want to stay with your brother?' asked the Doctor.

'You'll need me when the Sarns find out you've escaped from the cave.'

'I'll take care of the Doctor,' said Amyand, pointing to his sabre.

'There's not much you can do against laser guns,' said the Doctor's companion, rolling up his sleeve. 'But if they see this...'

The Doctor stared at the brand on the boy's arm. 'Does everyone from Trion have that mark?'

'No,' said Turlough enigmatically. 'You have to be very special to wear the Misos Triangle'. Unwilling to continue the conversation, he led the way through the black fissure in the wall of the cave.

The Doctor noticed the smell of sulphur in the tunnel was now stronger. It seemed warmer, too. As they hurried on through the narrow cleft he tried to puzzle out what had happened to the Master that he should need Kamelion's help so badly.

'Perhaps he's into another regeneration crisis?' speculated Turlough.

'His current body must be good for a few more years yet,' said the Doctor, wishing heartily that the evil Gallifreyan was indeed near the end of his unnaturally prolonged life. 'No,' he added. 'There must be another reason.'

The Master knew that Kamelion was returning. He could feel the approach of his *alter ego*, together with the band of primitives who would swiftly release his TARDIS. He laughed at the good fortune that had brought him to Sarn. Not only was he to be reunited with his slave, but the TARDIS sensors indicated a transforming power on the planet beyond anything he could create in his laboratory. He peered into the viewer, eager for the arrival of his rescuers.

The crocodile of Sarns wound along the ridge path like pious Athenians on the Sacred Way to the Acropolis. So much walking in one day had exhausted the Elders, but the Outsider would not let them rest. Peri, still in the savage grip of the automaton, glanced anxiously in the direction of the volcano, now venting continuous black smoke.

Timanov entered the ruin, gasping for breath, but he forgot his discomfort as soon as he saw the blue box—a most remarkable object. To his surprise, the Outsider gave the divine transporter hardly a glance, going directly to a pile of masonry in the far corner. 'Beneath that rubble,' he announced, 'is an object of incomparable value. A gift from Logar,' he added quickly, remembering the orthodox susceptibilities of his labourers.

Inside his TARDIS laboratory the real Master was busy bracing his equipment for the lifting of his precious column.

Outside, the Sarns toiled to move the many tons of rubble and stone that had collasped on the Master's time-machine during the earthquake. The children scavenged the small bricks and debris whilst the women conveyed away the light stones in a human chain, the men levering apart the heavy blocks and pillars, to reveal at the bottom of the heap a yellowing, Corinthian column with a door in the side.

'A pillar of stone?' cried Timanov in dismay.

'A TARDIS!' The Kamelion-Master smiled with satisfaction. 'I am most grateful.'

Peri was now very worried, for there was still no sign of the Doctor and Turlough. If she was abducted by this Master, her chances of seeing New York again were nil. 'You realise this creature is about to do a bunk?' she said, trying to stir up trouble between the Master's robot and the Chief Elder—only to wince with sudden pain as the steel hand of her captor tightened around her wrist.

But Timanov, who was growing more and more suspicious of the Outsider's strange behaviour, needed no promoting from the American. 'The Outsider will not leave without rewarding his faithful Sarns,' he warned.

The metal Master gave him an icy smile. 'As my word is my bond, Chief Elder, this is the day of reckoning for us all.' He took a step towards his TARDIS as the strongest men of Sarn began to haul on the ropes they had attached around the top of the column.

Inside, the Master clutched the metamorphosis projector as he felt the whole laboratory shake, then tilt like a beached yacht yielding to the incoming tide. Slowly the room revolved until floor, ceiling and floor were, once more, in their rightful positions.

'At last!' The Kamelion-Master surveyed the upright column with immense satisfaction, and tugged Peri towards the door.

'Don't let him escape!' screamed the girl.

'Where are the gifts?' protested Timanov angrily, little suspecting that both Outsider and stone pillar were about to disappear into thin air.

'Gullible idiots!' The robot Master laughed in the face of the disappointed Elders and dragged the struggling Peri through the entrance.

'We're too late!' cried Turlough, running into the ruin with the Doctor and Amyand, just in time to see the door of the Master's TARDIS slam shut.

The Doctor was already running towards the blue police box. 'I'm going to materialise around him,' he shouted as he ran. But he had reckoned without six angry, disillusioned Elders, who were less than mollified to see three prisoners from the cave at liberty, and were about to assault the great box. They rushed to the Doctor's TARDIS, laser guns at the ready.

Pushing Amyand and the Doctor between himself and the police box, Turlough turned to face the old men. 'It is the will of Logar that you obey me,' he announced in a grave voice. 'Put up your staves, for I am your new Chosen One.' He raised his arm in a Nazi-style salute to display, on his underarm, the brand of the Misos Triangle.

There was consternation amongst the Elders. Could the mantle of the dead Malkon really have fallen on this heretic? Timanov examined the embossed triangles. It was beyond doubt the authentic mark of Logar.

'What are you waiting for?' Turlough nudged the Doctor towards the TARDIS door.

'The box is sacred to Logar,' protested Timanov. 'It may not be profaned by his enemies.'

'The Doctor is no enemy,' replied their self-appointed leader. 'He is the rightful custodian of the box.'

The Elders continued to hold the Doctor and Amyand in their sights, though they dared not point the deadly lasers at Turlough, for no one dared kill a second Chosen One.

'Who is this Doctor?' asked Timanov, still suspicious of the young man by the box.

'He has been sent to help you. You have been cheated by the false Outsider.' Turlough stepped forward in front of the lasers and pushed Amyand and the Doctor into the TARDIS. 'Will you compound the murder of Malkon by defying your new leader!' he shouted, hoping no trembling finger would pull the trigger.

As Amyand stared in wonder at the interior of the TARDIS control room, the Doctor hastily replaced the comparator and set the co-ordinates that would reconfigure the TARDIS around the nearby column, while Amyand, via the scanner screen, watched Turlough haranguing the old men.

The Doctor glanced up and saw his worried look. 'We only need a few moments and the TARDIS will provide a spectacular diversion,' he explained as he activated the the dematerialisation control, where-upon the column shook and shuddered and corrus-cated with lights. Amyand was frightfully impressed, but not so the Doctor. 'We're stuck!' he cried, diving under the console. 'Oh, no,' he wailed, his head inside the pedestal. 'The temporal limiter has been disconnected.' He got wearily to his feet. 'Another old trick of the Master!'

'Just like the Doctor's,' said Peri, looking round the Master's control room.

'But infinitely superior,' sneered the Kamelion-Master. 'As I am to that galactic philanthropist.'

'I have computed the source of the power,' came the voice from the laboratory. 'Set these co-ordinates.'

As the automaton began pressing buttons on the console, Peri stared at the screen where she had seen the Doctor and Turlough arrive at their police box. Her heart sank, as the barrel in the centre of the room began to rise and fall and the image disappeared from the viewer. Revelling in her dismay, the robot Master produced a round object from his pocket and, with a sadistic laugh, explained how the Doctor's machine was inoperable.

The column was still, and a new view appeared on the scanner. While Peri peered at the gloomy cavern on the screen, wondering to what infernal region the creature had transported her, the metal Master left the control room, to return staggering under the weight of a large box which he placed on the floor beside the console. Peri could just perceive a faint humming above the ambient noise of the TARDIS. 'It's your control box, isn't it?' she said disparagingly. 'Forward, reverse, stop, like a toy train.'

'Very perceptive, my dear,' the Kamelion-Master replied as he opened the double doors. 'But the real power of my control is well beyond your inadequate comprehension.' The mocking smile left his face as he produced a sinister, black tube. 'No more childish heroics, if you please,' he advised as he directed her to the entrance.

They appeared to have arrived in the Hall of the Mountain King—or at least, thought Peri, in his boiler room. Everywhere, in the massive cathedral of a cavern, were ducts and conduits, cables and pipes of all sizes and shapes. Tubes and flues zigzagged across the walls and under gridded floors. At one side of the cave a column of fire rose from a vent, right up to a chimney in the high, rock roof. There was a continuous rumbling all around them and the floor vibrated like the deck of an ocean liner.

'Where are we?' said Peri nervously.

'In the heart of the volcano.' The Master waved her towards a large control desk on a raised dais.

Peri stood her ground. 'Look, if I'm to help you I want to know what you're doing and what happens to me when...'

'You will obey me without question!' the Kamelion-Master interrupted angrily.

'You said that once before,' Peri answered smartly back, hoping to regain mental superiority over the robot.

But the girl had more than the evil will power of the Master to contend with. 'Perhaps you doubt the efficacy of this device,' said the automaton, raising the black object. He turned to the wall of the cave where Peri could see three silver suits and helmets suspended from supports in the rock. 'Allow me to demonstrate the Tissue Compression Eliminator'. There was a red glow. First one, then another of what Peri took to be space suits, started to shrink, smaller and smaller, until each was a miniature of itself, fit only for a doll's wardrobe. 'The same will happen to you, my dear,' threatened the Master as Peri followed him obediently to the central control desk.

She looked at the views of the valley below the volcano that appeared on monitor screens set into the desk. At least the Master hadn't taken her very far. She could even see a speck of blue in the distant ruin— the Doctor's TARDIS!

The robot laughed when he realised what she was looking at. 'A modest thunderbolt, I think!' He pressed a lever and there was a distant rumble. The Kamelion-Master zoomed the picture in to give a closer view of the police box. Peri could hardly believe her eyes. The Doctor's machine was shaking, while debris rained down from the surrounding colonnade. The Master had precipitated an earth-quake!

The man in the black suit smiled. 'The entire power of the mountain is under my command,' he announced casually, as he started to remove a panel from the desk. 'Enough of games.' He knelt beside the desk and indicated that Peri should help slide back the metal casing. 'I am here for more serious work.'

After a moment of appraisal the robot proceeded to connect and reconnect various units and modules, some of which he removed entirely and handed to his pressganged assistant, before replacing in a different configuration. Peri shuddered to think what fearful power he intended to unleash.

The Master grunted with satisfaction and crawled out of the desk, the Tissue Compression Eliminator still firmly in his hand. He began to programme a keyboard on the edge of the desk. There was a gentle singing sound from across the cavern. The corona of flame from the vent had turned blue.

'Excellent!' the Kamelion-Master watched the plume of phosphorescence with great satisfaction. 'We now have control of one of the greatest energy forces in the Universe.'

'A blue flame?' said Peri, unimpressed.

'Numismaton, my dear,' said the Master-figure excitedly. 'An immensely rare catalyctic reagent from deep inside the planet.' The singing died down and the flame burned bright and hot once more. 'A mere test burning,' observed the robot. 'When the full surge comes, I shall be ready to absorb its infinite transforming power!'

'And I shall be transformed into a very dead Peri,' thought Peri, suspecting that the Master would soon find his young assistant irresistibly dispensable. For a moment the metal Master had relaxed, and stood complacently admiring his handiwork. The Tissue Compression Eliminator had drooped in his grasp. It was now or never. Peri decided she enjoyed being the size she was far too much to risk grabbing the weapon. Perhaps she could create a diversion . . . She leaned forward over the complex controls and ran her hand wildly over the knobs and buttons as haphazardly as a kitten dancing on the piano keys.

The Master snarled with rage and would have killed her instantly, but he needed to repair the sabotage. As the rumbling and roaring echoed through the cavern, Peri darted from the dais, across the cave and behind a large metal chimney.

For several seconds the Kamelion-Master was totally occupied calming the mighty giant that Peri had awoken. As soon as the power was checked, he reached for the Tissue Compression Eliminator to put an end to the child's impudent pranks.

A red glow shrivelled a pipe beside Peri's hiding place—the robot was after her. She could see, in the distance, an entrance to the cave, but she would never make it alive. She dodged behind another rank of pipes. The Master fired, missing her by centimetres, then strode from the control desk to flush his quarry from cover.

Peri dropped to her knees and crawled behind a ventilator unit. She peered out. Directly opposite, the Master's TARDIS offered the only possible sanctuary. She leaped forward, expecting at any moment to feel the annihilating glow of the Master's vile device.

'Peri!' shouted the robot, unable to fire without hitting his own TARDIS.

Peri reached the door, and without so much as a

glance back at her pursuer, ran into the control room. She had carefully memorised the switch for the doors and immediately pressed her hand to the lever, praying the Master hadn't operated any override. The whir of the servo-mechanism that closed the doors in the face of the enraged robot was the most beautiful sound she had ever heard.

It was several moments before she became aware of the angry buzzing from the entrance. Was the creature operating some cut-out that would open up the TARDIS to him? Or was he in the process of breaking in by sheer force? To her dismay, the noise grew louder.

Peri caught sight of the cabinet on the floor beside the console—the robot's control box. If only there was a way of immobilising the metal Master . . . That would serve the creature right. A puny mind, indeed. Well, she didn't have to be Albert Einstein to find the off-switch. She grabbed the side of the cabinet and began to wrestle with the lid.

Nothing could have prepared Peri for the horror of the next few moments. The top of the box came off in her hands exposing the interior of a doll's house TARDIS and a Tom Thumb man, dressed in black velvet. The lilliputian peered up into the light that flooded down into his diminutive compartment. And Peri gazed at the ratsized face of the real Master.

The miniaturised Time Lord stared at Peri from his shrunken laboratory. 'You escaped from my slave,' he squealed at the terrified girl. 'But you will obey me or die!'

10

The Blue Flame

The Doctor was in despair as he saw the Master's
TARDIS dematerialise on his scanner screen. 'We've
lost him! he shouted.

'And your friend Peri,' said Amyand sadly.

'And my temporal limiter,' bemoaned the Doctor,
in the certain knowledge that he could neither follow
the American who had saved his life, nor, with the
TARDIS immobilised, save himself and Turlough
from the doomed planet.

'But where's he gone?' Amyand couldn't take his
eyes off the empty corner of the screen from which the
yellow column had inexplicably vanished.

'I don't know!'

A flashing light in the corner of the console
attracted the Time Lord to a little known control
unit. 'Someone's been interfering with the TARDIS
navigation system,' he exclaimed. He peered at the
setting which Kamelion had selected. 'It's been
remote paralleled with the Master's TARDIS!'

'I don't understand,' said Amyand in a fairly
massive understatement of the general culture shock
he had experienced walking into the blue box.

'Perfectly simple,' said the Doctor, beginning to
look more cheerful. 'The two TARDISes are
programmed to follow each other. We could follow
the Master if he hadn't removed my temporal
limiter.'

'You know where he is?'

'Indeed I do.' The Doctor double-checked the
unlikely reading. 'He's still on Sarn.'

'But why?'

'There's something the Master needs, here on this planet.'

The Doctor looked up at the screen where Turlough was arguing with the old men. It seemed as if his companion was going to need some help. He grinned as an idea came to him; with the help of the TARDIS, he could put the fear of god into these primitives. 'What does Logar look like?' he asked Amyand.

Although an Unbeliever, Amyand had as clear an idea of the Fire Lord of Sarn as an Earthchild of the mythical unicorn. He had lived with the images and inscriptions and old people's tales as long as he could remember. 'Large, silver, like a man...' he began.

The Doctor thought for a moment, then programmed the data bank. An awesome Greek bronze appeared on the screen. 'One of Logar's Earth equivalents,' explained the Doctor. 'Poseidon rising from the waves.'

'Not quite right,' said Amyand. 'The Fire Lord of our legends is fatter, squarer-headed. Not so many features.'

The Doctor entered some corrections and the picture on the screen began to resemble the young Sarn's description.

'That's more like it.'

An alarm sounded in the seismic sensor and a deep vibration shook the TARDIS. 'Must be another earthquake,' said the Doctor, switching back the screen to a view of the ruin. As they watched the tumbling masonry, he breathed a sigh of relief that his police box had materialised at a safe distance from the toppling walls.

'Where's Turlough?' cried Amyand, seeing no sign either of the boy or the six Elders.

The Doctor pointed towards the door. 'Prepare to receive visitors.'

One by one the old men filed in behind Turlough, peering round the control room in myopic amazement. 'Sorry, Doctor,' said Turlough. 'There was nowhere else I could bring them.'

He decided not to tell the Doctor how much he had enjoyed playing the little nabob. He had given the Elders a right castigation for shooting his brother, called them all the names in the book and threatened them with their own fire. Finally, the mere mention of creating rival Elders from among the common citizens had brought the quaking Timanov to his knees in a fulsome protestation of loyalty. Turlough was rather disappointed when the earthquake made them seek shelter in the police box.

'Welcome, gentlemen,' said the Doctor, smiling.

His worthy guests looked curiously at their young host.

'This is the Doctor,' announced Turlough. 'He is not an enemy of Logar, but an Elder of the city of Gallifrey.'

'Do any of you recognise this?' asked the Doctor, casually pressing a key on the desk. There was a mighty roar, overlaid with a fanfare of synthesised trumpets and a dazzling icon of the Fire Lord appeared on the screen. All the Elders fell reverently to their knees. 'The image of Logar!' cried Timanov reverently.

'You see,' hectored Turlough. 'He appears at the Doctor's command.'

'Why does he not strike down the heretic?' The Chief Elder pointed to Amyand.

'Logar is the friend of all people,' catechized their new Chosen One. 'He is only angry when the citizens fight among themselves.'

The old men shuffled closer to the scanner to marvel at the likeness on the screen. The Doctor, too, was wondering, as he gazed at the silver figure, whether the beast on the scanner was as mythical as he had previously supposed. 'Does that image remind you of anything?' he whispered to his companion.

Turlough examined the computer-generated picture for a moment. 'A man in a thermal suit?'

The Doctor nodded. 'Timanov,' he addressed the Chief Elder. 'Have you ever seen Logar?'

'Yes,' replied the old man, humbly. 'When I was a boy.'

'Where?'

Timanov was silent for a moment before he replied. 'Near the summit of the Fire Mountain.' There was angry murmuring from the other men and a surprised cry from Amyand. The Chief Elder had climbed the forbidden slopes!

Timanov smiled gravely at the Unbeliever. 'You see, I too was once young and hot-headed. But the Fire Lord appeared to me. He was merciful, and I was born again.'

The Doctor looked at Turlough. They both had a pretty good idea what lay behind the Chief Elder's Damascus Road conversion. 'A vulcanologist!' exclaimed the Doctor. 'We know the old Trion colonists used volcanic power in the city. They must have another control centre right inside the volcano.'

There was a bleeping from the console; the seismic scanner had been activated again. 'Not an earthquake,' said Turlough, peering at the unit.

'That's odd,' said the Doctor. 'Something must be happening inside the volcano itself.' He rushed to the door.

The smoke had cleared from the top of the volcano. A pale blue fire burned above the crater. 'It's an eruption!' shouted Turlough.

'I don't think so,' said the Doctor.

The Elders, who had followed them out of the

TARDIS, viewed the shimmering phosphorescence around the mountain top with wild enthusiasm. 'The blue fire has not been seen for many generations,' said Timanov, trembling.

'What does it mean?'

'It is a sign of great favour,' replied the Chief Elder. 'Logar shows his mercy to the sick and injured.'

The Doctor was thinking back to another blue flame, guarded by the Sisterhood of Karn, whose power had helped many a Time Lord to regenerate. If the same force was available in the mountain it might explain why the Master had lingered on Sarn.

'We must return to the Hall of Fire,' cried Timanov. 'There will be a great gathering.'

Amyand sighed. 'More superstitious ritual.'

The Doctor didn't agree. There was nothing superstitious about the Trion colonists who built the Hall of Fire and installed the gas control system— presumably to utilise some volcanic potency. 'Come on!' he yelled, starting to run after the Elders who were already hurrying back along the ridge path towards the city.

'Where are we going?'

'The Hall of Fire. I want to analyse the deposit on the wall of the cave.' He paused. 'Unless, of course, you can *tell* me what it is?'

'How should I know?' said Turlough. 'That cave's part of a colonial civilisation that ended ages ago.' He moved to follow Amyand along the path, but the Doctor dragged him back. The Time Lord wanted a few words in private with this young man who knew a great deal more about Sarn than he liked to let on.

'That volcanic control system has been used in living memory. Just what sort of interest have your people got in the stability of an abandoned planet?'

'I don't know.'

'I think you do. When you arrived you expected to

find Trions here. And what about the ship? What was your father doing here? And your brother? And just what are you afraid of, Turlough?' The Doctor fired question after question at his evasive companion.

The boy blushed and stammered. 'Please, Doctor. Not now. I'll explain later.'

The Doctor wondered how far he could give him the benefit of the doubt. 'Just one thing, Turlough.' He turned the boy roughly towards him. 'If you're withholding any information that is going to help the Master, then our friendship is at an end!'

The Master was not a man used to making mistakes, and he had cursed himself repeatedly for the positively schoolboy error that had all but cost him his life. He had long wanted to improve the Tissue Compression Eliminator, and his inspired modifications would have increased its range and power a hundredfold, to make it the most sophisticated and deadly weapon of its kind in the whole universe. The first experiments had been entirely successful, and it was not until he powered the prototype on his laboratory work bench that the misphasing of the proton accelerator became apparent.

Although he had experienced a somewhat alarming sensation—fatal to anyone but a Time Lord—he was not immediately aware of the scale of the disaster, as the laboratory itself was reduced proportionately. It was only as he tried to leave the workroom that he realised he was but a fraction of his former self, trapped and impotent in a giant TARDIS. But his mind was unimpaired, and, indeed, he had quite redeemed his carelessness with the ingenuity of his system for remote-controlling the time-machine, and the expertise with which he had constructed the metamorphosis projector.

Across time and space he had called to his slave, and, from the very **TARDIS** of the unsuspecting Doctor, Kamelion had come to his rescue. His familiar had even brought him to this planet, and the undreamed of power of numismaton.

No machine would be needed to counter the disastrous effect of the Tissue Compression Eliminator. The blue flame would not only restore him to his former stature, but would infinitely extend his fourteenth incarnation. Out of failure had come success, from calamity he had snatched the supreme triumph of his career... Until that wretched girl interfered!

The roof of his laboratory had been ripped off, blinding the Master with the arctic glare of the control room light. He peered upwards as the massive moonface of the girl rose over the grey, roundeled wall. She stared down into the tiny box, like a rich, spoiled child wondering which doll's house inhabitant to lift out and torment. The one helpless inmate of the workroom grabbed the fatal prototype of the Tissue Compression Eliminator and brandished it at the giant Peri.

'You will obey me or die!' he repeated at the top of his little voice.

Peri recoiled at the sight of the soft-suited homunculus in the box. She was sickened and revolted at the spectacle of a perfectly formed human reduced to the size of a half-grown hamster. She dropped the lid and pushed herself backwards from the cabinet. So sharp was the movement that the box toppled over onto the floor of the control room.

The unexpected reversal of his little house caught the diminutive Master unaware, and he was ejected from the container like a human-cannon ball. He lay for a moment stunned on the hard, grey plain of the floor. As he recovered his senses, the midget Time

Lord could see, to his right, a great, white horizon of wall that stretched upwards to infinity, and to his left an unassailable, basalt cliff of console, while in the foreground loomed the mighty crag of one of Peri's shoes.

The Master got to his tiny feet and looked round for shelter. About a hundred yards away was the mouth of an enormous cave, where the lid of the box lay against the side of the console. The Master sprinted across the open ground and into the protecting darkness.

Peri looked down at the scuttling creature on the floor and began to feel her courage return. She took off her shoe; not the most sophisticated weapon, but against this little noddy-man it was the equal of the Tissue Compression Eliminator. She snatched away the lid and the wretched Master was exposed like an earwig beneath a stone. He scurried once more across a floor the size of a football pitch to where, in grander days, he had piled some cable against the TARDIS wall. He reached the safety of the huge coils just as the hammer heel of Peri's shoe crashed to the floor inches behind him. He lay panting amidst the strands and hawsers which stretched round him like the chains of some nightmare suspension bridge. But there was no time to rest. He got up and raced along the narrow canyon between the cable and the TARDIS wall before Peri could expose him yet again.

Peri bided her time, the deadly shoe raised over her head. Her prey broke cover, but not where she had expected and the little man was halfway across the floor before she saw him. She hurled the shoe, and missed. She ran forward, but the Master had reached the sanctuary of the console and had disappeared through a cable duct in the base of the pedestal. Peri knelt in front of the tiny aperture, like a cat beside a hole in the skirting board.

The Master stood quaking in the warm darkness. Above him, components shone like stars in a night sky, and, as his eyes adapted to the light, he could make out the shapes of a thousand gigantic chips and transputers. The air was full of strange sounds: the hum, the buzz, the rattle of the million secret parts used to control a time-machine.

An ominous shadow hung over the entrance. It was that terrible girl. 'Peri! Peri!' cried the Master. 'Listen to me!' Peri lowered her head towards the faint but insistent voice inside the console. 'There is no way you can escape, either from my TARDIS or the control centre.'

'We'll see about that,' said Peri, picking up her shoe.

'Peri... Miss Brown. Help me, and I will spare your life.'

'Oh, sure. I know how much your promises are worth. I'd rather wait for the Doctor.'

'The Doctor!' The Master cursed his old enemy, and looked around his hiding place. He recognised one of the outsize units above his head and hauled himself up onto a nearby block. From there he clambered, like a boy chimney-sweep, up the narrow shaft between two panels. Panting, he reached a flat landing of printed circuit. All he needed was a conductor to short-circuit two of the strips and the way would be open for Kamelion to rescue him from that girl. He plucked a silver thread from his collar and pressed it to the board. There was a distant clunk from one of the servos. The Master laughed.

Peri was getting anxious. It was far too quiet inside the console. She jumped to her feet at the sudden whirring. The double-doors had opened and the Kamelion-Master would be through in seconds. She rushed to the inner door.

'Kamelion!' screeched the impatient Master.

'Kamelion?' whispered Peri, from where she had paused in the corridor.

Neither of them could see the minuscule metamorphosis projector, on its side and out of control beside the fallen laboratory.

'Kamelion?' said Peri, more confidently, and tiptoed across the control room and out through the double doors.

Kamelion lay, a fizzing wraith of himself, on the rock floor outside the Corinthian column. Peri came to the entrance and smiled. 'Pleasant dreams,' she murmured, and stepped over the paralysed robot, out into the cavern. She ran to the tunnel entrance she had spotted earlier, hoping it would lead to the open air and a path down the mountain, back to the Doctor.

The Doctor scraped with his spatula at the sticky rock wall of the sacrificial cave in the Hall of Fire and examined the slime in his pocket microscope. 'Just as I thought. Trace elements of numismaton.' He looked up at Turlough. 'Very useful to a Time Lord who can't regenerate!'

There was a shout from the Hall and Sorasta came running from the portico as the Doctor and his companion emerged from the cave. 'Doctor, Malkon is much worse.'

The Doctor nodded. He had expected as much. Though Turlough's brother had escaped being killed outright, the Time Lord feared, as soon as he had examined him, that the boy who had prevented his own execution was dying.

'We must get him to the TARDIS,' pleaded Turlough.

'No.'

'Doctor, please!'

'Thanks to the Master, he's better off here,' said the Doctor dashing out of the Hall.

Malkon's racing pulse was weaker, his breathing more shallow and he had a fever. Roskal stood up from where he had been kneeling beside the bed as the Doctor clattered down the stairs of the bunker. To the surprise of the young Unbelievers, the visitor did not immediately examine his patient, but went to the controls of the machine.

'There is a healing power in one of the volcanic gases,' he explained. 'That's why the old Trions constructed the Hall of Fire. Some sort of curative centre.' He began pressing buttons on the panel. 'We need to release the gas flow—strictly for medicinal purposes.'

They came to the Hall of Fire from all over the city: the maimed, the diseased, the crippled, the blind. Amyand was appalled as he watched the sick people of Sarn carried up the steps into the Hall.

'Don't stop them,' said Turlough, as the invalids gathered round the cave.

The Elders now entered, following the injured to the mouth of the grotto. Timanov smiled at Turlough. The new Chosen One had indeed brought them the favour of Logar. 'The gift of the Fire Lord.' He bowed and handed the Doctor's companion one of the finest trinkets from his own secret treasure store. Turlough looked thoughtfully at the shining object—he had handled one of those many times before.

They were all distracted by a sudden roar from the cave. The flame burned brightly once more.

'Excellent,' said the Doctor running up the steps.

'That flame will burn,' protested Amyand angrily.

'Just a residue of hot gas,' said the Doctor, hoping it wouldn't take too long for the discharge of numismaton to reach them from the volcano.

There was a murmur from the crowd and all eyes turned to the entrance. Amyand and Sorasta had appeared at the top of the steps carrying the lifeless body of their former Chosen One. Turlough ran to join them and helped move his dying brother to the group of sick and wounded around the cave entrance.

Everyone in the Hall now stared into the raging flames and the Doctor prayed that he had pressed the right switches back in the bunker. Without any warning, the roar in the grotto died away. There was a hush amongst the waiting wounded and their families. The heat haze in the cave cleared to reveal the dark, stained rock. There was a gentle hiss like summer rain on a pavement and the walls were shrouded in a luminous white vapour. An eerie singing echoed in the cave as the cloud turned blue.

'Pure numismaton,' said the Doctor, peering at the waving phosphorescence. He nodded to the Elders. 'It's quite safe.'

Timanov gave the sign for the gathered sick to enter the cave, but the sad little group lingered by the platform, nervous and overawed by the shimmering presence in the grotto.

'What are you waiting for?' cried Turlough, and, taking his brother in his arms, walked across the platform and into the electric radiance. Encouraged by his example, the sick and the wounded of Sarn stumbed forward into the light.

Afterwards, Turlough could remember very little of those moments of rare unction in the rocky cell. There was no sense of time or space, but only the certain knowledge that all things were well.

The Doctor's companion was the first to leave the brightness—alone. The crowd gasped as the boy was followed by his brother Malkon, pale and amazed, but walking upright. Behind them came the other Sarns, miraculously restored to health, to be embraced by their weeping families and friends.

'Praise be to Logar!' cried Timanov.

The Doctor was silent. He, too, was moved by the power from the mountain, yet dreaded how the healing force might be abused by the Master. The release of numismaton could have been no coincidence as there had not been a Gathering for two generations. This surge had been precipitated by the Master, and with scant regard for the stability of the planet. At least he now knew where to find him.

The ground trembled and the volcano rumbled angrily, a reminder of the terrible danger they all were in.

'Assemble the citizens in the Hall of Fire!' ordered Turlough, in a loud voice. For a moment Timanov hesitated. 'Logar demands it,' the boy cried.

The Chief Elder gave a small respectful bow. 'Of course, Chosen One,' he replied obsequiously.

The Doctor looked towards the volcano. Somewhere near the crater he would soon confront his old enemy. 'Can you guide me up the mountain?' he asked Amyand. 'The seismic control centre must be near where Timanov saw the vulcanologist.'

'Ready when you are, Doctor,' said the young Sarn, who had not expected a return journey to the peak quite so soon.

'Once I've got the TARDIS working we'll materialise here and take the Sarns on board,' the Doctor explained to Turlough, wondering how he was going to cope with so many passengers.

'That won't be necessary,' said his companion, holding up the piece of engraved silicon given to him by the Chief Elder. 'This keys the transmitter on my father's ship and gives me direct access to Trion Communications Executive. They can send a transporter.'

'Couldn't be better!' The Doctor was delighted not to have to live in a time-machine full of evacuees.

Turlough sighed. He was relieved to have made the decision, but frightened of the consequences. As soon as he gave his rank and identification number, the Custodians would be after him.

'You *are* in trouble, aren't you?' The Doctor spoke very gently to his companion.

Turlough nodded. 'I should never have escaped from Earth. My ten years' exile was not complete.'

'Exile?'

'You see, Doctor, there was civil war on my planet. Revolution against the Imperial Clans. We were defeated... Barbarians!' he muttered, scornful of the new egalitarian regime that had sent him from his homeland. 'My father was condemned to death, but the sentence was commuted. Transportation to this old prison planet.'

'This was a prison planet?'

'Yes,' explained the disgraced Trion. 'When the colonists left it was not immediately abandoned. For several years it was a penal settlement.' He pointed to the mark on his arm. 'You see, Doctor, the Misos Triangle is the brand of a criminal.'

They left the city together: Turlough, with Roskal for moral support, to go to the forbidden lands and locate the crashed ship's powerful transmitter, the Doctor and Amyand to climb to the mountain control centre where the Master had his hideout.

As they walked through the outskirts of the settlement, Turlough talked bitterly of his exile on

122

Earth. 'I was sent to learn the ways of another planet. What can an Imperial Trion learn from Earth people?'

'Humility?' suggested the Doctor, rather astringently, wondering what sort of monster his companion would have become, had he continued to be brought up as the scion of an aristocratic, ruling family.

Turlough said nothing, knowing that his burst of arrogance had offended the Doctor. He felt a bit ashamed. The Doctor saw the boy blush. 'Are you sure they'll know you've absconded?' he asked, more kindly.

'Oh, yes. There are Trion agents on every civilised planet. An agrarian commissioner on Vardon, a tax inspector on Derveg,' Turlough grinned ruefully. 'And a very eccentric solicitor in Chancery Lane, who had me incarcerated in that ghastly school!'

The tiny, black body of the Master lay on the wide TARDIS floor, like a cock-sparrow downed in a high wind. The rebel Time Lord was exhausted. For a brief moment, he even believed himself to be doomed. Why had the slave not answered his summons when the doors were opened?

At least that girl had left the control room. The thought of Peri breathed new life into him. To have been defeated by the Doctor, his Gallifreyan peer, would have been humiliation enough; to be destroyed by an Earthling, a mere girl, an American even, would make him the laughing stock of the Universe! He must not give up now.

Slowly, he dragged himself across the endless Sahara of floor, till at last he reached the overturned laboratory, and hauled himself onto the wall which was, once again, the floor of his miniaturised workroom. Immediately he saw the reason for Kamelion's delay. The metamorphosis projector had been damaged. The Master ran to inspect the vital equipment. To his profound relief, it was not beyond repair. Soon, his other half would revive and carry him to the blue fire. He would regain his former stature; he would be stronger than any Time Lord, he would be indomitable.

Turlough and Roskal wished the Doctor and Amyand good luck as they parted in the fertile valley where the Sarns had their fields. It was not far over the ridge into the forbidden land, but the going was difficult as the earth tremors were getting more severe, tumbling loose rocks from the hillside and sending up great, choking clouds of lava dust. 'Come on!' shouted Turlough, above the ophicleide thunder of the volcano. 'The ship!' He pointed to the horizon.

Roskal half expected to be apprehended by Timanov's guards as they walked up to the shattered leviathan. Such trespass was the greatest crime a Sarn could commit. He followed Turlough to the intact flight-deck section, whilst all round them the structure creaked and groaned like a galleon under full sail.

'Look out!' yelled Turlough as a girder from the deck above them crashed across their path. 'We haven't got much time.' He knew the layout of the ship by heart and went straight to the transmitter.

'Is it still working?' shouted Roskal over the rattle of the twisting hull.

'Soon see,' said Turlough, feeding the coded release key into its housing. 'Keep your fingers crossed.'

For a moment nothing happened, and Turlough

124

was beginning to wonder if the emergency power cells had dissipated their charge, when two green lights flashed. He quickly entered a password on the keyboard and waited anxiously while the volcano roared again. 'I hope there's not too much geo-magnetic interference,' he muttered.

His doubts were dispelled by a distant voice from his home planet. 'Trion Control. State name, rank and identification code.'

The boy froze. He was about to sign the warrant for his own inevitable rearrest. His hand went bravely to the transmit key. 'My name is Vislor Turlough, Junior Ensign Commander...'

Rescue would soon be on its way for the stranded Sarns. But for Turlough, there was now no escape.

The Doctor and Amyand climbed higher and higher up the quavering mountainside. It was a hard struggle against the sliding shale and drifting pumice, while the sulphurous smoke caught in their throats. The Doctor paused for breath and looked down at the black panorama of cinders and tufa in the valley below him. He imagined how Sarn must have been in the days gone by: a colonial paradise with the forces of nature held in check by the technical ingenuity of the Trion settlers, until nature started to get the upper hand, and the soft life of the expatriots became threatened by a native force no army from the Imperial Clans could ever pacify—the volcano.

But while Sarn might have been too hot for the wealthy colonists, it was an ideal dumping ground for undesirables from the home planet. The Doctor described to Amyand how his forbears had been brainwashed Trion dissidents, abandoned to fend for themselves amongst the territorial leavings of the

Clans; how new arrivals were dumped, mindless in the forbidden lands, and left to wander into the city where they were received as gods by the superstitious tribal community that had sprung up. 'You see only prisoners fresh from Trion would have the Misos Triangle,' he explained.

They began to climb again. 'The entrance to the control centre should be somewhere near here,' said the Doctor. 'This must be where Timanov saw the vulcanologist.'

Amyand imagined the effect of the silver engineer on the young Sarn. And he was beginning to understand the passionate faith of the old men. Outsiders *had* come at the Time of Fire—to control the volcano when it became critical. The technicians would have brought gifts—food, tools, supplies of all kind for the prisoners and their descendants. 'But why did they stop?' he asked puzzled.

'Cuts, I expect,' said the Doctor. 'They needed to pay for a war or two in their other colonies.'

'Will they want us back on Trion?'

The Doctor laughed. 'I expect the new regime will treat you like heroes.'

There was another loud rumble from the mountain, this time deeper and more sustained. The black smoke grew thicker and the crater above them glowed red. 'We're too late,' cried the Doctor.

A thin, crimson tongue of lava gently licked over the volcano's peak. Slowly, but inexorably the flaming stream oozed down the mountainside. The ground throbbed. Smoke and steam and asphyxiating gases burst from the earth all about them. The noise was ear-splitting. The Doctor and Amyand staggered to a halt, retching in the poisonous air. The way ahead was blocked by the flaring cataract. Already the heat was unbearable.

'We'll have to go back,' yelled Amyand.

They turned to retrace their steps. But as they retreated it seemed to get hotter. The reason was soon only too horrifyingly obvious; another all-consuming, incandescent cascade of molten rock poured from the crater, trapping them between two widening streams. The Doctor looked round for a way of escape. Directly below them the two lava flows were about to join together. They would have to go up and hope to find the entrance in the mountain before it was too late.

The ground immediately above the path was almost sheer, but there was a small ledge about ten feet above them. Amyand climbed onto the Doctor's shoulders and tried to haul himself up. But the porous rock crumbled in his grasp. He tried again, setting off an avalanche of pumice which poured on top of them. The little island between the two lava flows grew smaller. The heat was now almost unbearable. The Doctor tried to push Amyand further up...

'It's no good, Doctor,' cried Amyand, sliding back yet again.

'Doctor! Doctor!' There was another voice somewhere, in the smoke above them. The Doctor peered up and saw Peri's grimy face looking over the ledge. She leaned down and grabbed Amyand's hand. The young Sarn scrambled up, and taking off his tunic, used it as a rope to haul up the Doctor.

'Quick,' shouted Peri. 'Over here.' She led the way along the ledge and into a narrow opening in the side of the rock.

They lay on the floor of the tunnel, exhausted, while smoke and fire blotted out the entrance behind them. It was the second time the American had saved the Doctor's life, and it was lucky for all of them she had been unable to find her way off the ledge and down the mountain before the eruption.

Peri herself was delighted to be reunited with her friend from the police box. The Doctor would be able to deal with the Master and his Tin Man; then they would all escape in the other travelling machine. She quickly recounted her adventure with the lilliputian Master. 'He's still inside the TARDIS,' she explained as they got to their feet and hurried along the tunnel. 'Running about like a rat in a hayloft.'

'He must have had an accident with the Tissue Compression Eliminator,' exclaimed the Doctor, glad at last to know the nature of the Master's incapacitation. He grinned mischievously. There was a delightful irony in his old enemy being so perfectly hoist with his own petard.

'Why wasn't he killed?' asked Peri, who had seen for herself the devastating effect of the little black twig.

'Must have escaped the full impact. Besides, he's a Time Lord.'

'A Time Lord?' Peri was wondering just what race of supermen she was dealing with.

The rocky corridor led them straight to the seismic control centre. 'A masterpiece of Trion engineering!' whispered the Doctor as he surveyed the machinery in the cavern. He spotted the only too familiar yellow column and ran to it. In the doorway lay Kamelion in an unrecognisable heap, fizzing peacefully. 'Keep an eye on him,' said the Doctor to Amyand and raced to the control panel in the centre of the huge cave.

'Where are you going?' cried Peri, who had expected the Doctor to hunt the Master in the TARDIS.

'I must slow down the eruption!' shouted the Doctor. 'The Master's interference has unstabilised the seismic machinery.' He began, tentatively, to adjust the position of some of the levers. 'If I override the automatic controls I might be able to delay the

128

worst of it.'

'Can't you stop it?'

The Doctor shook his head. 'The Master has already triggered a massive surge of numismaton from the planet's core. When that hits the surface it will disrupt the inhibition system altogether.' He glanced at one of the monitor screens with its view of the city in the valley below. 'There will be devastation.'

Gradually, the Doctor learned how to generate a counterforce of the volcano's own energy that could check the discharge from the magma chamber. The fragile equilibrium established, the rumbling grew less aggressive. The Doctor checked the readings and scanned the monitor screens. He breathed a sigh of relief: the lava flow had petered out. 'That should hold back the eruption for a while. Long enough, at least, for the Sarns to escape.' He followed Peri towards the yellow TARDIS. 'Now for the Master.'

Amyand looked up from his vigil over Kamelion's shimmering body. 'No change, Doctor.' The Doctor nodded. It seemed the Master had lost control of his only friend. He led the way into the Corinthian column.

The cabinet was still lying exactly where it had fallen, but the Doctor went straight to the console and began to strip out one of the components. 'Exchange is no robbery,' he murmured as he removed the temporal limiter with which he could repair his own machine. 'Now for the laboratory,' he whispered, and tiptoed towards the cabinet, keeping clear of the open side. As soon as he reached the miniaturised compartment he seized it and turned it upright, as if it was a snare containing some wild animal.

The Doctor gasped as he peered over the little wall. He had not prepared himself for the shock of seeing his old enemy so cut down to size. Could that really be the supreme adversary, whose evil purposes he had thwarted across the centuries: that little doll in the velvet suit?

The minuscule Master got, once more, to his feet and scowled up at the giant Doctor, who loomed over his laboratory, flanked by an equally massive Peri and Amyand. 'So what does it feel like to have a taste of your own medicine?' boomed the Doctor.

'I live, Doctor!' piped the pygmy Gallifreyan in shrill defiance.

The Doctor felt an unworthy thrill of pure vindictiveness. 'Albeit in somewhat reduced circumstances,' he jeered at his humiliated rival.

'I shall soon be restored,' boasted the little man. 'To profit from my research.' Without turning his head from the Doctor's gaze, he swivelled his pinhead eyes towards the metamorphosis projector he had finished repairing the second before his laboratory had been righted. 'Come, my Kamelion,' he whispered under his breath. 'Revive! Revive!'

The Doctor squinted at the matchbox workbench. 'You were experimenting with the Tissue Compression Eliminator.'

'To increase its power a hundredfold.'

'You made it too powerful for your own good.'

'A small design problem.'

'And a very small Master!'

The elfin figure clenched his little fists, wishing he had annihilated the Doctor in the Hall of Fire.

'That's why you needed Kamelion, isn't it?'

The Master sneered at the Doctor who had so naively trusted the silver factotum. 'I have lodged in the mind of that slave since our fateful meeting on Xeriphas.'

The Doctor remembered Kamelion's extraordinary seizure back on Earth. 'The scream in the TARDIS.

He even *felt* your pain.'

'And came instantly to my help!' The Master began to laugh. 'Now with the next surge of numismaton, all is prepared for my supreme renewal.'

'Kill him!' cried Amyand, amazed at the arrogance of the evil pixie. But the Doctor did not move. 'What are you waiting for?'

The Master knew the Doctor better than the militant Sarn. 'Just as he has waited for centuries,' he mocked. 'Second rank genius crippled by moral scruple. How could the Doctor ever destroy *me*!'

Amyand did not appreciate the nicety of a rhetorical question and gave an immediate answer. 'By wringing your neck as if it were a rat or a snake. And if he won't do it, *I* will!'

'No!' screeched the Master.

'Out of the way, Doctor.' Amyand pushed the impotent Time Lord aside. 'I owe you a favour.'

The Master screamed like a gin-trapped rabbit as the huge, red, calloused hands came down on him. He recoiled from the unnatural body heat, gagging at the stench of the enlarged sweat glands. He wriggled furiously as the young man's fingers curled around him like the coils of an enormous boa constrictor.

'Away from the box!' A familiar voice sounded from across the control room.

The Doctor, Amyand and Peri swung round. Standing in the doorway, Tissue Compression Eliminator in his hand, was a full-sized Master.

11

The Time of Fire

As Turlough hurried back towards the city, he was relieved to see the eruption had stopped. The Doctor must have reached the seismic control centre and would soon have his TARDIS working. The boy was tempted to escape in the police box from his appointment with the Captain of the Trion personnel carrier that would soon be landing. But he decided he had been a fugitive long enough. Ex-Ensign Commander Turlough would obey the orders he had just received from Executive Control.

'You saved our lives.' Roskal tried to reassure his sad companion. 'They can't punish you after that.'

'Just so long as they don't send me back to Brendon,' replied Turlough, smiling bravely.

'Is that a prison?'

'Far worse!' he groaned, thinking back to the cold showers and compulsory games of his *alma mater*. 'It's an English Public School.'

Kamelion, once more the Master's familiar, laughed at the dismay of the Doctor. 'For a fleeting moment I was in your power,' he jeered. The robot's human hand tightened on the Tissue Compression Eliminator.

'I hardly need to remind you what will happen if you use that thing in here.' The Doctor gave a meaningful look around the TARDIS control room to the Master's diminished laboratory.

'That will not be necessary.' The robot waved the Doctor, together with Peri and Amyand, out through the double doors.

'He's let us go!' exclaimed the American as they emerged from the Corinthian column.

But the Doctor knew the cruel Time Lord had intended no mercy. 'He needs to take the TARDIS into that circle of flame.' He pointed to the corona on the other side of the control centre, where the fire rose through the cavern from a grid in the floor. 'When the next surge comes he'll be surrounded by the restorative gas.'

'But you've removed that limiter thing. His TARDIS is stuck.'

The Doctor explained how the Master could replace the missing component with the same part he had previously stolen from the police box. But at least there would be a few moments before the yellow machine was operational—time to organise their own escape. The Doctor took the newly acquired temporal limiter from his pocket. 'Amyand, go back with Peri and give this to Turlough.'

'Look!' Peri pointed to the flames now burning in the entrance tunnel.

The Doctor groaned. 'Gas must have seeped in and ignited.'

'We're trapped!'

A flash of silver beside some wall lockers caught the Doctor's eye. 'Thermal suits! Those Trion vulcanologists have just saved our lives.'

'One of our lives,' corrected Peri. 'Two of these things are for midgets.'

But the Doctor, running across the cavern, had already spotted the single intact kit beside the miniaturised clothes. 'Don't worry. So long as one of us can get the limiter back to Turlough, my TARDIS will do the rest.'

'*You* must go,' said Peri, picking up the silver suit.

'No,' said the Doctor, opening out the protective

fabric. 'I've got some modifications to do to that control unit.' He turned to the Unbeliever. 'Your turn to play Logar, Amyand.'

The young Sarn was soon transformed into the same god-like silver figure that the Doctor had conjured up for the benefit of the Elders in his TARDIS.

'Good luck!' shouted Peri, as the Doctor closed the helmet.

Amyand smiled bravely and began to plod across the cavern in the direction of the tunnel. He paused for only a moment before plunging into the flickering fire.

The Doctor was already kneeling by an open panel in the side of the control desk with several components in his hand.

'What are you doing now?'

'Trying to raise some local radiation.' He pulled one of the units apart. 'If I can induce a sympathetic reaction in Kamelion's psycho-circuits he'll have an electronic heart attack.'

There was a grinding sound from across the cavern. Peri stared in disbelief. Though she had now travelled inside two TARDISes, she had never yet seen a solid object disappear into thin air. One moment the fluted Corinthian column was in the corner of the cave, the next it had vanished... To appear, she noted with alarm, in the centre of the corona.

The Doctor merely glanced up from the pieces of Trion machinery that he was now reassembling. The Master's TARDIS had materialised, just as he predicted, in the centre of the circle of volcanic fire. He turned to Peri. 'When I give the word, push that control hard to the end stop.' He pointed to a sliding lever on the console. 'Now, get down behind the desk.'

Inside the chimney of fire, the Kamelion-Master stepped from the yellow TARDIS, the precious casket in his arms. He placed the reduced laboratory containing the injured Master in the centre of the grid and peered through the surrounding curtain of flame. The Doctor, he observed, was tampering with the seismic controls. 'Get away from there, Doctor!' he shouted.

Peri hugged the ground, her heart pounding, while the Doctor worked on, ignoring the orders from the corona.

'I shan't warn you again,' cried the metal Master, raising the Tissue Compression Eliminator.

The Doctor seemed oblivious of the danger. 'The Master can't fire for fear of hitting the control system,' he whispered to Peri.

'He's a robot,' retorted the Doctor's terrified assistant. 'He'll just walk through the flames.'

'I hope so,' replied the Doctor. 'This device will only work at close range.'

'I've warned you,' called the angry robot again. He peered at the Doctor. The meddling Time Lord must not be allowed to tamper with the gas flow to the corona. The Kamelion-Master stepped forward to pass unscathed through the cordon of flame. He laughed. It seemed that the Doctor had forgotten his durability.

'He's coming,' hissed Peri.

'Keep down,' whispered the Doctor, as the facsimile Master walked slowly towards the desk. The black-suited robot chuckled. The moment of his supreme triumph would be enhanced by the elimination of the Doctor and that girl.

'Now!' shouted the Doctor, leaping from behind the desk with the hastily rigged weapon in his arms.

Peri jumped up from her hiding place and pushed up the slider. There was a high-pitched whine and the Kamelion-Time Lord uttered a terrible scream, half in the strangled voice of the Master and half with the tortured metal larynx of the automaton. The black suit and the evil features flared a dazzling silver while the arms of the creature flailed in a rabid death throe. Slowly the writhing shape became the robotic Kamelion. The vibrating machine-man collapsed to the floor.

'He's trying to say something,' said Peri, coming out of hiding.

The Doctor leaned over the palpitating factotum.

'Kamelion... sorry... no good,' announced the dying robot.

'I'm sorry, too,' said the Doctor sadly.

'Destroy me, please!' begged Kamelion.

'Get back!' yelled the Doctor to Peri as he picked up the Tissue Compression Eliminator that had been flung to the ground. He raised the black tube and pressed the activator, whereupon an orange glow concealed the master of disguise. The light dimmed, and the prodigy of Xeriphas was no more. A mere nugget lay, like a twisted tin soldier, on the empty floor.

Kamelion had been eliminated.

Amyand staggered up the steps of the Hall of Fire, utterly exhausted. The thermal suit had proved remarkably light in view of the degree of protection it provided as he walked, unscathed, through the fiercest flames, but it was a pity he couldn't get rid of it as soon as he left the danger area. The catch on the helmet had stuck and he needed outside help before he could shed his silver skin.

There had been no sign of life as he entered the city and it was a great relief to discover Turlough, still in the Hall of Fire, arguing with Timanov and a group of Elders. 'We're running out of time. You must leave for the landing ground!' Turlough's voice came, loud and clear, through the electronic ears of the helmet.

'Leave us in peace. We wish to end our days in the settlement. Strong in the faith.' Timanov was proving as intractable as ever.

'I order you!' cried the new Chosen One.

Timanov smiled proudly. 'Order the citizens as you will. I shall stay here and die with the Fire Lord.'

The old men turned towards the lumbering Amyand, who was about to ask Turlough to release him, when he noticed the look of rapturous awe on the face of the Elders.

'Logar!' cried Timanov ecstatically, flinging himself, with the other men, prostrate on the floor in front of the disguised heretic.

Amyand realised that he must look exactly like the young vulcanologist who had appeared to Timanov as a young man—he was probably wearing the self same suit. He was about to ask Turlough to release him when he saw the boy's frantic gestures. He smiled as he realised what was expected of him. 'Go to the landing stage!' His booming voice, relayed from the microphone in the helmet, echoed round the ancient Trion spa. 'It is the will of Logar!' thundered the *deus ex machina*.

The transceiver the Doctor had tried to repair chose that moment to crackle into life. 'This is Trion space carrier two zero fifty, Captain Lomand commanding. On final approach to Sarn.'

Clutching their pathetic little bundles, the people of Sarn waited beside the ruin where the Doctor's TARDIS had first materialised. They cowered as they heard the roar, believing that the mountain, once

138

more, was pouring out its fire. The noise grew unbearable, and the citizens feared that the earth itself might open up to swallow them, when they saw the great bird loom from the dark clouds.

The Trion ship had already landed by the time Turlough and Amyand arrived at the ruin. Turlough could see Captain Lomand talking to Sorasta while his crew began to organise the embarkation. The renegade ensign ran to the Doctor's TARDIS, clutching the temporal limiter he had just been given by Amyand. He hoped that no one would spot him, for with the Doctor stranded in the seismic control centre, there was no time for explanations.

It took him only a few moments to slip the limiter back into its housing. There was no need to set the co-ordinates as the remote parallel function, pro-grammed by Kamelion, would materialise the police box beside the Master's TARDIS in the cavern.

Turlough became aware of someone behind him. Finishing his work, he turned to the doors where a man in a grey uniform was watching him.

'It's customary to salute a senior officer, Tur-lough,' said Captain Lomand.

Turlough felt a surge of hatred for the Trion commander who had followed him into the control room. This would be one of the new breed of upstart officers who had hounded his father to death.

'Still running away?' said his fellow Trion.

Turlough glanced at Lomand. The man should know that an Imperial Clansman does not run away. 'If I was running away I would hardly have asked for a ship from Trion,' he answered coldly, activating the controls. He walked to the door and turned for one last look round the console room before addressing the Captain of the rescue ship. 'The TARDIS is on a time-delayed take-off. We have fifteen seconds to get clear.'

Peri watched the embarkation on the screen of the seismic control desk. 'Now that's what I call a space ship.' She pointed to the huge Trion vessel beside the ruin.

'Not much use to us,' replied the Doctor, without taking his eyes of the gauges on the console. 'The only way out of here is by TARDIS.' He glanced hopefully at the space where the police box should materialise. 'Come on, Turlough,' he whispered nervously, for time was running out. Nothing would hold back the surge of numismaton and the subsequent destruction of Sarn. Nor was there any way of preventing the renaissance of the Master, who lay secure in his laboratory, guarded on all sides by the impenetrable flame, and waiting for the healing vapour.

The cave began to tremble; pale smoke, smelling of joss filled the air. An ethereal singing came from the corona; and the flame around the Master's casket turned blue.

'It's the surge!' cried Peri.

Another blue miasma began to form beside the control desk. 'Well done, Turlough!' shouted the Doctor, as his TARDIS materialised. He pushed the young American towards the safety of the police box and turned to face his adversary, alone.

The pale blue phosphorescence played around the box in the corona. The head of the growing Master appeared like the rising sun over the wall, laughing with exhilaration as he felt the strength flow into him. The Doctor stared, appalled, at the evil genius rising from the cabinet. The Master saw his old enemy watching him. 'I shall come from this fire a thousand times more strong,' he cried. 'To hound you, Doctor, to the borders of the Universe!'

The Doctor was trembling. He peered anxiously at the control desk and back at the fiend who continued to grow inside the corona.

There was another confident, mocking laugh from the Master—and then a gasp. The blue of the numismaton was suddenly flecked with red and yellow. The Time Lord's leering smile twisted to a grimace. He screamed with pain. 'Cancel the reinjection immediately!'

The Doctor did not move.

The Master struggled to escape the flame, but could not stir from the corona. 'Doctor!' he howled. 'I will plague you for the rest of time for this...Agh!' A blood-curdling scream echoed round the cavern. The agonised Master stretched out his hands towards his enemy. 'Help me, Doctor, and I will give you anything in Creation!'

Every instinct in the Doctor urged him to cut the calorific gas he had fed back into the numismaton. He had never before wilfully inflicted such pain on another living creature, nor ever would again. In those dreadful moments, the Doctor suffered with his fellow Time Lord all the tortures of the damned.

'Please, Doctor!' The Master was weaker now. 'Pity me?'

The Doctor just stared into the flames.

The fire turned to sheer white, and, with a final withering scream, the Master disappeared from view.

The Doctor walked slowly across to his police box. Black smoke filled the cavern and lava began to seep through the cracking floor, as the TARDIS dematerialised.

'You okay, Doctor?'

The Doctor leaned trembling on the control room console. He turned, ashen, to the thoughtless girl. 'Do you realise what I've just had to do?' He checked himself as he saw her vulnerable, concerned face.

'Yes, of course I'm ... *okay*.' He grinned. 'Where's Turlough?

'Didn't show.'

The Doctor nodded and began to set the co-ordinates for the ruin.

The volcano was surrounded with fire. Lava poured from its sides and would soon engulf the city.

Turlough stood with his brother beside Captain Lomand, watching the last of the citizens file into the transporter. 'Am I under arrest?' he asked the officer.

'Do you want to be?' said the commander.

Turlough was hopelessly confused. Was the man trying to make a fool of him? Captain Lomand smiled. 'Things have changed on Trion since the days of the Imperial Clans. We no longer persecute our political opponents. You are welcome to return ...' He looked across to where the blue time-machine was reforming beside the ruin. 'Or not, as you please.

'Embarkation complete, sir,' shouted one of the crew.

Lomand glanced at the Fire Mountain. 'Time we were gone.'

Turlough looked towards the Doctor who had just opened the door of the old police box. 'Please, Turlough!' pleaded his new-found brother.

'Malkon, you board,' said Turlough. 'Go on!' he shouted and ran to the TARDIS.

'Do you need someone to put in a good word for you?' asked the Doctor, kindly.

The young Trion shook his head. 'My exile has been rescinded.'

'I'm pleased for you.'

Across the open space, Captain Lomand stood patiently beside the ship's ramp.

'I shall miss you,' said the Doctor.

'I don't want to go,' said his friend. 'I've learned so much. But there's Malkon... And I've got to return some day.'

The Doctor nodded. 'Better go back while you're a bit of a hero.'

Turlough smiled at Peri who had appeared in the doorway behind the Doctor. The cheery American would make an admirable companion. 'Look after him. He gets in the most terrible trouble.'

Turlough grasped the Doctor's hand. 'Thanks for everything.' He turned and walked smartly across to the waiting transporter. He paused for a moment, and looked back. Then, without a wave, he strode up the ramp and was gone.